Branch of the Talking Teeth

Other ROUSSAN junior fiction titles
by Ishbel Moore:

THE SUMMER OF THE HAND

THE MEDAL

Branch
of the
Talking Teeth

Ishbel Moore

Cover illustration by Janice Poltrick Donato

ROUSSAN
PUBLISHERS INC.

Roussan Publishers Inc. acknowledges with appreciation the assistance of the Canada Council and the Book Publishing Industry Development Program of Canadian Heritage in the production of this book.

Copyright © 1995 by Ishbel Moore

Legal deposit 2nd quarter 1995
National Library of Canada
Quebec National Library

Canadian Cataloguing in Publication Data

Moore, Ishbel L. (Ishbel Lindsay), 1954-
Branch of the talking teeth

(On time's wing)
ISBN 1-896184-06-5

I. Title. II. Series.
PS8576.06141B73 1995   jC813'.54   C95-900232-4
PR9199.3.M6187B73 1995

Printed and bound in Canada

To
my children
Brad, Ishbel and Elizabeth

and
Special Thanks
to
Jackie

Chapter One

Teta's breath caught in her throat as a shadow fell across her. He had come, at last. She closed her eyes to the sparkling water in the rock channel below, while the battering winds ran powerful fingers through her long, dark hair.

Carefully, so as not to fall over the rough, grassy edge, she turned and stood up. But she had been sitting for a long time and her legs had become weak. She stumbled and threw out her arms for balance. The strong grip of the stranger's right hand steadied her. She breathed deeply, then, rubbing her palms together, raised her eyes.

He wore braided leather footwear and leggings that ended beneath the yellowish-white covering of a great snow bear. The bear's rear paws trailed on the ground. Its sharp front claws, no longer a menace, hung over the stranger's bony shoulders. His delicate-looking fingers wrapped around a carved walking stick. White hair whipped across his blue eyes and about his pale, young features. The muzzle of the great snow bear lay on his forehead. He and the animal appeared to be one.

"Moonhead," Teta whispered. It was neither a statement nor a question.

He nodded.

"I'm Teta," she said, aware of an uncomfortable warmth in her cheeks. He was like no one she had ever seen before, and not as frightening to look at as she had expected.

"I was sent to wait for you. My father, Lome, is honoured that you have come." Teta signalled to Moonhead with a curl of her pointing finger. "Follow me."

She picked her way down the steep, rocky incline. There was no set path. Each time she or her father ventured out, they climbed or descended from a different starting point. Lome would not risk having his cave discovered nor, as he continually pointed out, herself, his cherished daughter.

Halfway down, she turned and waited. She stared at the beads of sweat on Moonhead's forehead, his free hand clutching his side, and realized that he had been hurt. She wondered fleetingly about helping him, but then he glared at her. Teta lowered her eyelids and continued on.

Below, the ribbon of sparkling water lay edged in bluish-grey sand. The sheer points of the Island of the Birds loomed where the channel emptied into the grey sea. Teta smiled. She loved how the island gleamed white in the sun, while the gulls and auks screeched overhead. Beyond the pointed rock, where the sea thundered, hovered the mist—always present, always threatening to turn to fog, always a danger.

Moonhead cried out and tiny rocks skittered between Teta's feet, causing her to whirl. He slid a short distance. Instinctively, she reached for him, just as he had helped her moments before. This time he did not glare at her. Teta nodded and grinned, and picked her remaining steps more slowly.

Lome emerged from the deep curve of the cliff face. A smile spread across the corners of his weather-beaten face as he gestured to Moonhead to sit. Moonhead grimaced and gingerly lowered himself onto the sand.

"I knew you'd come," Lome stated. "You're hurt. Soogat?"

Moonhead nodded.

"You're no doubt hungry and thirsty," Lome said. "Teta prepared you some food earlier this evening."

Without waiting for her father's nod, Teta entered the deep curve and returned quickly. She handed Moonhead an ivory cup of sage tea and a shell plate of seaweed and fish. She caught a glimmer of gratitude in the wary face.

"How did you know I would come here?" Moonhead asked.

Teta found his accent heavy, but the lilt in the voice was intriguing.

"I told Mukta to send you," Lome said, still smiling. "When I heard about your... em... arrival and your growing status among the South People, I knew it would only be a matter of a few seasons." Lome squinted down the channel and out to sea. "After Bugt died during the snow time, I wondered how Soogat, his son, would handle your popularity."

"Yes," Moonhead said quietly, "but I do not understand why I must run only to fight."

"It's the way of the people of the Land of the Blue Rock," Lome answered, looking steadily into Moonhead's puzzled face. "When the chief dies, his son takes his place. But, once in a while, the people prefer another as leader. The chief's son must then order his challenger out of the settlement without food or weapons. He's allowed two days' and two nights' lead. Meanwhile, the people eat sparingly and drink only water to clear their heads. At sunrise on the third day, the chief's son can start out in pursuit."

"Soogat follows me. I can sense it." Moonhead sighed. "Why could we not settle this face to face?"

"Ah, well, you see, it's not often that a man alone and with

9

no weapons survives in this place—between the cold, the animals, the fog, and the cliffs," explained Lome. "That man must live by his wits. If the chief's son catches up with him, they usually fight to the death, or until one gives in. The victor then decides whether or not to kill his opponent or banish him. The strongest, smartest, and fittest man becomes the new leader."

"I've been told," Teta interrupted, desperate to change this dark subject, "that you possess a story-tree."

Moonhead nodded again, but did not look happy.

"I've heard that you bring joy to those who listen," she added. "Is it true that you comforted Bugt in his last days with a tale of what lay ahead for him? Did you really charm old Aurtoo with your ideas?"

Moonhead squirmed. Her interest made him uncomfortable.

Lome cleared his throat to silence his daughter.

"Forgive her," he said, "she means no harm. She's young and I've kept her with me too long. But I didn't want to see her bonded with Soogat as was her mother's wish."

"Soogat has talked much about you," Moonhead replied, looking hard into Teta's eyes until she blushed. "I know he plans to take you back with him when he is... er... finished with me."

"Mukta will see that Soogat waits the two suns before following you," Lome continued. "He wounded you to slow you down. Tonight we'll tend to your needs and prepare you for travel."

He paused, his lips pursed in thought. Teta watched him closely as he stared at the seals playing in the evening waves.

"Teta and I have talked about this often," he said. "She'll go, too."

"No," cried Teta. "I can't leave you! You never told me you would stay behind. Soogat could kill you."

"I agree," said Moonhead. "I have already travelled two whole days. I can only move slowly, and Soogat begins tomorrow." Moonhead groaned as he got to his knees. "No. I must travel alone."

Lome smiled sadly. "I'll bond you before you go so that Soogat cannot mate with Teta, even if he catches you."

"You think you have this all planned, old man," Moonhead said coldly. "I do not think I want to bond with Teta. I do not know her, and I am only ten plus six summers."

"Teta's two summers younger. It is time," Lome stated, firmly. "Many of the South People her age are already bonded and have children by now. Futhermore, it's not customary to refuse the gift of a wife. It's also not customary to contradict an elder."

"Is it customary to run away with another man's bride?" Moonhead replied, sounding just as angry but much more controlled.

"Ah, Moonhead," sighed Lome, sinking onto a nearby rock, "you're right to speak so. But Soogat, as you know only too well, is not a gentle man. When my wife, Kaatka, made the bargain with Mutka that the two babies should bond when grown, I protested strongly. Even the great silver wolf howled when Soogat's first cries were heard. That was a bad omen."

Lome sighed again and rubbed his hands together. "The weather cycle following his birth was the coldest and hardest I've ever lived through. I never liked Soogat, even as an innocent boy. Never. He has a... a burning in his eyes."

"I have seen that burning," Moonhead said, quietly. "But he

was not always unkind. Not to me anyway. When I was first pulled from the sea, it was Soogat who tended me when Mukta was too busy or too tired. It was he who held my head so I might swallow better."

"Huh," snorted Lome. "It must have been to his advantage. He was probably using you to prove to his father that he could be caring."

Teta thought Moonhead wanted to argue but Lome kept talking.

"No, Soogat is not a pleasant man," he said. "That's why I left the winter settlement when Kaatka died two weather cycles ago. I didn't want my daughter spending her life with him. I've heard you're kind and wise. I would have her bond with you."

Teta shivered. The thought of bonding with Moonhead, strange in ways, strange in speech, and full of strange stories, chilled her bones. But bonding with Soogat, whose burning eyes and bad temper she remembered well, chilled her more. The sea wind blew colder.

"She'll be a good companion to you," Lome stated, leaning toward Moonhead in encouragement. "She knows this land as well as any. And she'll lead you to the safety of the North People."

Moonhead met Teta's eyes. She stared back, noting the way the rising moon made his fine hair glow against the dark rock.

"I will consider this," he answered quietly.

"So will I," Teta threw back at him across the sand.

She wasn't sure she liked the choices. She could stay here with Lome, knowing that eventually she would have to return to her people. But by then she would be an old woman—with no children to care for her.

She could acknowledge her mother's promise and live with Soogat. She would be wife of the chief. By custom, he would have to consult her on matters regarding the health and well-being of the people. But living with Soogat also meant enduring his tantrums and his touch.

Or she could bond with Moonhead, a man she knew only from Mukta's gossip during her rare stolen meetings with her father—how Moonhead had been pulled from the sea just before the great rock channels filled with winter ice by Bugt and Soogat. How he had come in a vessel from far away, the only survivor.

"I'll think about it," she repeated, returning Moonhead's cold glare.

Lome laughed. "You young people have no respect for the elders. But I like your spirit. Soon you are going to need it. Come," he chuckled, "come into the cave."

Teta watched as Moonhead rose to his feet with the aid of his walking stick. Pain turned his already white skin almost blue. He took a shuddering breath and followed Lome into the cave. Teta was keenly aware of the importance of the cave's entrance hidden in the crevices. By carefully placing a few well-chosen boulders, she would prevent Soogat from learning their whereabouts.

Lome eased Moonhead onto a bed of grass and caribou skin. He then made a fire with his flints and oil in a central fire pit. In moments flames illuminated the cave.

"Rest," Lome ordered gently. "Show me where it hurts."

Moonhead placed his walking stick on the dirt and shrugged out of his bear covering. Lome helped him remove a thin caribou-hide vest, leaving only a loin cloth and his leggings. Moonhead carefully manoeuvred onto his side and groaned.

Teta gasped at the jagged wound stretching from Moonhead's armpit to his waist.

He untied a braided thong from around his chest and clutched an object which Teta could not quite see in the dimness. As Moonhead moved, the object made a clattering, chattering sound and came plainly into view. Teta's mouth fell open.

Six human teeth dangled from a slightly curved stick.

This had to be the story-tree.

••••••

Soogat paced up and down in front of his people. Every now and then he would stop, growling and shaking his head as if angry at the air in front of him.

Mukta and other older members of the the South People followed him with their eyes. They, too, often growled and shook their heads, but they were angry with Soogat.

The young men sat across the camp looking very uneasy. In response to Soogat's earlier orders, some were sharpening their spear points. The sound of stone against stone smacked in time with Soogat's pacing. He reached for the spear tied on his back and fingered the point. It was made of rare black obsidian, harder and sharper than flint.

"Sit down," Mutka shouted. "The darkness won't pass any quicker whether you walk or sit. You know that at sunrise you can start out after Moonhead."

Soogat growled at her. "Yes, old mother. And I know you sent him to Lome, wherever that is. Why?"

"For you own sake," she answered, "because the People may not have forgiven you if you had killed him."

Soogat marched around the ring. His stomach churned with impatience and would not let him settle. His mother's words echoed in the wind. *If you had killed him, killed him.* He laughed out loud, ignoring the nervous glances of the young girls and elders. He could have killed Moonhead easily, at any time. Moonhead was a scrawny weakling who had no wish to fight, even for sport.

Soogat could still see the fear in Moonhead's eyes as he had slashed that white skin. A niggling sadness bit at Soogat's heart. They had been friends once—in the beginning. He raised his head to the gathering stars and laughed again to crush his weakness.

He stopped in front of his mother.

"You gave him the white bear," he said. "That was supposed to be mine when I became leader."

"*If* you become leader," she shot back.

"*When* I become leader!" He shook his fists at the lengthening shadows. "If only Jaanu, our Woman of Wisdom, hadn't died. Then Moonhead could never have wormed his way into the hearts of the People, and I'd be leader by now."

"If you don't become leader it will be because you aren't worthy, despite your blood ties," Mukta said. "Even Jaanu was limited in her powers. But she might have been able to argue with Moonhead, or battle his stories with our own."

Mukta looked around the ring of silent villagers. "It still makes me shiver to hear how our forefathers followed the hairy beasts over the stretch of land now under the faraway sea. We need to find a new Wise One and soon." She wagged her finger at her son. "You have not proven your strength against the great animals, or pitted your own nature against the wilderness."

"I know that, old mother." Soogat hunched down in front of her. "I was about to begin my journey when *he* came."

A smile spread over Mukta's face. "Moonhead was given to us by the sea."

"I was there when his vessel was hauled out of the waves. I should have pushed him back in and let the Sea Goddess keep him." He started pacing again.

Aurtoo, one of the grey-haired women beside Mukta, poked her in the ribs with her elbow.

"What a story Moonhead told about the beginning of stars," she said. "Let me see. How did it go? Oh, yes. *In the beginning, everything was dark and silent. The dark and silence grew and grew until it burst into a great shower of stars.*"

"Enough," cried Soogat, annoyed at the way even his hunting men were listening intently. He was sick and tired of these stories. "Everybody knows it was Mother Creator who made the stars. Moonhead is suffering from some sickness of the head."

"What harm is there in listening," Aurtoo piped up. "The tales give me something to think about."

"Then maybe you should be thinking about a new leader," Soogat whirled on her. "Storytellers and dreamers don't make good leaders."

"But we like him and trust him," Aurtoo replied, smiling innocently.

Soogat felt anger and frustration rising in his gut. He grabbed Aurtoo by the hair, forcing her to look up at him.

"And you don't like me or trust me!" he yelled. "When Moonhead is gone, I'll spend my life proving that I am worthy of being your leader. The storytellers will never tire of retelling the tales of Soogat, the handsome, brave, and strong leader of the South People."

Mukta kicked out at his shins. He yelped and let go of Aurtoo.

"You treat an Old One like this and then say you're worthy?" Aurtoo hissed. "I don't think so. Oh, you're strong and handsome. Moonhead, though, he's beautiful to look at," she paused, "and brave in a quiet way. But you? I question *your* bravery."

Soogat raised his hand to strike her. Mukta caught his wrist. Her face was twisted as if in pain. He felt her disappointment.

"Stop this!" she cried. "Or you might never become leader."

Soogat wrenched his arm away and stomped toward his hut.

Chapter Two

"Is that the story-tree?" Teta asked, no longer able to contain her curiosity.

Moonhead shook the branch. Rattling noises filled the cave.

"Ooh," cried Teta, falling on her knees beside him. "What kind of thing is it?"

Lome stood behind and peered down. "It has teeth hanging from it. Why? What do they do?"

Moonhead held the branch higher. Happiness spread over his features and glowed in his eyes, as if warming him from the inside.

"It is called the Branch of the Talking Teeth," he explained. "I took it from one of the men who died while we crossed the sea. He was a true storyteller."

"What happened to the others?" Lome asked, wiping the blood off Moonhead's skin with wet moss.

Wincing, Moonhead shifted his gaze from Teta.

"One by one, my father, my uncle who was the storyteller, and my older brother died. I don't know why I did not die. I was the youngest and weakest. I should have died first. Instead, I lived on, eating food meant for them."

"Your life had a greater purpose, Moonhead," Lome said, creasing his brow as if the thought weighed heavily on his mind. "Under the power of the Goddess of All, your people had to die so that you could come here, to us."

"To do what?" Moonhead grumbled. "Bring trouble and

disorder to the People? Perhaps bring death to you and your daughter!"

"Where did the teeth come from?" Teta prodded in an attempt to chase away the fear growing inside her heart.

Moonhead ran his fingers down the row of teeth, making them rattle on their braided strands.

"One tooth belonged to each of the storytellers who carried the branch before. Each is attached by hair from those storytellers."

Teta leaned closer. She pointed to the last tooth, the one closest to Moonhead's hand. "This one looks very new."

"Yes," Moonhead replied, growing more somber. "My brother plied it from my uncle's mouth before we gave him to the sea."

"And strung it to the branch with some of his braided hair." Teta grinned, proud of herself for understanding.

"But why?" Lome repeated. "And how does it make stories?"

Moonhead, with help from Teta, managed a sitting position. Then, with a delighted laugh, he shook the Branch of the Talking Teeth.

"Each storyteller became known for a particular tale. Each tooth therefore tells that story." He looked at Lome, choosing his words. "It is a way of remembering stories. The ancient storytellers still talk by way of the teeth. Teeth are in the mouth. Words pass over teeth as they make their way into the ears of listeners. The Branch of the Talking Teeth is now the mouth of the dead storytellers."

Teta felt her skin crawl and yet she longed to know more about the six back teeth dangling from the wood—wood made shiny-smooth by much touching.

"Do you remember all six stories?" she asked.

Moonhead exhaled and shrugged.

"I do not remember all the stories in complete detail. I only remember what every child is taught by listening to the story-tellers." He gazed into the fire. "You see, I was not chosen to be the next storyteller. It was to be my brother. My uncle was teaching him all the tales, so I only listened with one ear."

"Yet you're much loved by the South People for your stories and kindness," Lome soothed as he patted Moonhead on the shoulder.

"What did your people call you?" Teta asked.

He sniffed and rubbed the back of his hand across his nose.

"Mearanach," he replied. "It means 'struck by the moon.' My mother always complained that I would sleep all through the day if she let me and stay awake all through the night. When I came to the settlement of the South People, Soogat asked me my name. We could not understand each other and so we used our hands. I pointed to the moon and then to my head, and Soogat thought my name was Moonhead. I never bothered to change it."

"I think Mearanach died on that long sea voyage with the rest of his kin," Lome said. "Moonhead, the storyteller, belongs to the history of the Land of the Blue Rock now."

He placed a moss pack under a baby sealskin on Moonhead's ribs and bound it with sinew.

"Where did you get that white bear fur?" Teta asked, coming closer. She itched to touch the story-tree. Her father waved her back.

Moonhead turned his face to the fire which Lome now

coaxed into greater heat. Smoke disappeared into the unlit regions.

"Mukta gave me the bear fur as I was leaving," Moonhead replied wearily. "She told me it was a great prize and insisted I take it. When she told me how to find you and your father, she kept saying she hated to see her true son and her new-found son fighting each other. I worry about what has become of her."

"Do not fear for Mukta," Lome added. "Soogat won't drive out his own mother. The South People would not allow it."

Teta settled into a cross-legged position beside Moonhead. Despite the uneasiness in her breast, she felt drawn to this mysterious man whose white skin burned orange in the firelight.

"Who can you pass the stories to?" she asked.

"The person must be related by bond or blood," Moonhead said sadly. "I am alone here. I fear the stories will die with me."

Lome jumped in excitement. "All the more reason to bond with Teta now. The bonding can serve the dual purpose of saving your stories and, hopefully, your life. It also releases Teta from her mother's pledge to Soogat."

Teta clasped her hands over her mouth to keep from crying out. Would she be able to remember the stories of some faraway people? Would Moonhead have enough time to tell them to her before Soogat caught up? The responsibility made her squirm.

Then Moonhead spoke, interrupting her racing thoughts.

"I do not seem to have any choice," he sighed.

Teta's stinging retort died on her tongue. A man was supposed to be glad to be given a mate. Soogat would have been. She swung her gaze from Lome to Moonhead and back again. Twice she opened her mouth to speak, but nothing would come out. She found herself entranced by the Branch of the Talking Teeth.

As they sat in the deepening darkness, she became aware her life was already linked to Moonhead's. At that moment Teta realized she wanted, no, *needed* to go with him—bonded or not.

♦♦♦♦♦♦

Soogat chewed at the inside of his cheeks and stared at one of the four hairy beast tusks which supported the skin roof of his hut. Several notches had been chipped into one—a notch for each weather cycle that had passed since his mother and Kaatka had pledged him to Teta. There should have been only ten plus two, but because Lome had taken her away, there were ten plus four. That was two whole weather cycles longer than any man should have to wait for bonding.

He flung himself onto his fur bedding, face up. He traced his fingers along the notches.

"Oh, Teta," he whispered. "I haven't forgotten you. No other mate will do for me. I have turned away from many inviting smiles, my little one, because none can smile like you. I'd hoped you would return before this, but you haven't. So, I'll come looking for you."

He chuckled, deep in his throat, and rolled over.

"Thanks to my old mother, Moonhead will find you for me. He knows he's no match for me. Surely, when he and I meet, he will give in, and I can banish him forever. Then, you and I, Teta, can be together."

Soogat sucked air in through his teeth. Images of victory swam in his mind.

Chapter Three

"Stay close to the shore," Lome cried in warning as Teta and Moonhead set out the next morning. "That way great bear and wild cat can't sneak up on you."

Teta raised her hand as a sign that she had heard and trotted after Moonhead.

"I do not understand why I am running away from Soogat," Moonhead growled as he tapped the earth and rock with his walking stick.

"To prevent him from killing you," Teta replied earnestly.

"He will catch me sooner or later," he continued.

"Not if I can help it," Teta cried.

"Oh, Teta," he groaned, stabbing angrily at a tuft of spiked grass. "You know better than that. Soogat is not going to rest until he finds me and secures his position as leader of the South People. With this wounded side, I cannot travel very quickly."

"When we get to the North People," she began.

"*If* we get to the North People," Moonhead shook his head. "What can they do? Hide me? Fight Soogat? I do not believe they can help me."

"So why did you leave the South People and come to us? It would have been just as easy for you to wait for Soogat," she countered, glancing at him sideways.

"Soogat forced me to leave. He pushed me over the first hill himself." Moonhead gestured the action with his hands. "I... I do not know what kept me moving."

Teta scanned the horizon while she gave herself time to think. Although she could not yet see it, she knew that in the distance the ice water glittered blue and behind that loomed the Great Snow Wall. The North People lived on the shore of this Blue Water.

Teta had been to the Land of the North People many times with her father. She loved to watch the way the sea pounded at the Great Snow Wall, breaking off pieces into floating ice rocks. The old people said that the snow wall was melting and moving north and feared that their children's children's children would not see the snow wall at all.

She looked back and saw her father standing on the cliff edge. The sea and the sky met in a thin line beyond. Gulls squealed in the winds above.

Last night, Lome had made her hold hands with Moonhead. He had then placed the Branch of the Talking Teeth over their heads and spoke about the power of the sea and the wind that brought them together. He expressed the hope that Moonhead would give Teta the gift of his stories and that she, in turn, would pass them on to future generations—if something bad should happen to Moonhead.

Moonhead had been very quiet after the unusual bonding ceremony. He had turned toward his side of the hearth and fallen asleep. Teta had tossed and turned all night.

♦♦♦♦♦♦

"Maybe the time it takes us to reach the North People is meant for you to teach me the stories," Teta said to Moonhead. Her gaze followed the ragged coastline, her mind locating the next of Lome's well-hidden caves. Ice hills drifted south on the grey sea.

"I do not know where to start." Moonhead stuck out his bottom lip and adjusted the slate point harpoon Lome had given him.

"Mukta always said that if there's something to say, it should be said from the beginning," Teta said, side-stepping a small boulder no doubt left by the melting snow wall. The snow wall did that—left little crushed rocks or piles of huge boulders or sometimes the remains of a frozen hairy beast, whose tusks were great rewards for the finder.

"Humph. I know that Mukta always had something to say herself," Moonhead said, checking over his shoulder. He strode on, his walking stick hitting the ground every fourth step.

Teta decided his wound must not be hurting so much any more. She tried to match his speed. None of the South People, or the North People, for that matter, ever walked with such long spaces between steps. At this pace, they'd leave Soogat far behind.

Glancing at Moonhead, she could see he was gathering his words. She kept quiet.

"These stories, as well as I can recall them," Moonhead said with a serious look, "do not explain why the skies rumble during a storm or where the rainbow comes from, as your legends do. They are told to help pass the long, dark hours, and perhaps there is a message in them for the people listening. Every family tries to keep its own Branch of the Talking Teeth, you understand."

Teta nodded, her breathing shallow.

Moonhead pulled out the Branch of the Talking Teeth. The

teeth rattled under the force of his walk. He pointed to the one farthest from the hand grasp. It was smaller than all the others.

This is the story of the first tooth—the tooth of Isma. Isma was beautiful and wise. She lived in a land of high mountains and many animals. She was always watching the animals and learning their ways. She loved them all, but her favourite was the fast runner.

Teta laughed. "A fast runner? What's that?"

Moonhead shook his head. "I am not sure. We do not have fast runners on my island. I have been told, though, that it has four legs, a strip of hair on its long neck, and a hairy tail. They are not very big, but can run like the wind and are nice to look at. My uncle said that some men have tried to get on their backs!"

"Oh! I'll try to see one in my mind," Teta frowned.

Moonhead took a deep breath and continued.

In this mountain-land the men were fierce and angry at each other all the time. One, named Cabul, shared his hearth with Isma. Cabul was the leader of many fierce men. Isma had much trouble with Cabul. He was always taking his men and fighting with nearby tribes. They mainly fought over the fast runners which were their chief source of food. One night, while Cabul was fighting, Isma had a dream.

In the dream, two very big fast runners, both males, one white and one red, came to fight each other for the females and grazing-land. It was a frightening dream. The fast runners stood up on their hind legs and struck with their sharp hooves. They screamed and snorted and stamped, kicked and pushed with their heads. They bit each other without mercy and the blood ran down their coats until the grass was stained red. The fast runners fought on for many hours until both fell to the ground, dead.

With no leaders, the rest of the fast runners scattered throughout the mountains where other vicious animals killed them.

When Isma awoke the next morning, it was to hear that her hearth mate and the leader of his enemies had both been killed. For what, she asked herself? Some land? Some food? The battle had no real purpose. There had been plenty for everyone.

Isma, because of her dream, knew that another leader had to be found before the lesser leaders came down from the mountains. She gathered her courage and proclaimed herself the leader. Thus, she looked after the two villages for many years, living in peace and teaching others the futility of war.

She often said that she would rather have all her teeth pulled than use them in battle. But men, being as they are, rose up against her. Those loyal to her cause found themselves fighting. Isma was killed by her own nephew, Behing, who had all Isma's teeth pulled out.

Behing's sister, Shalag, stole one of the teeth and attached it to this branch. The branch is from the tree that used to shade Isma from the hot sun.

That is the story of the first tooth, the tooth of Isma. I send heartfelt thanks to Isma for her story.

"Isma was a wise woman," Teta said, clapping her hands with delight. "I think I can see in my head what fast runners look like."

"I hope you will be able to remember the story," Moonhead stated flatly as a large hare scampered into the nearby bushes. "I will tell the same story another two times and then you repeat it to me three times."

"By then it'll be time to stop and eat," she snorted and held out her hand.

Moonhead looked at her outstretched palm. Without even slowing his pace he asked, "What do you want?"

"To hold the branch," she answered simply.

"No," he snapped. "Not until it is your turn to tell the story."

On they walked, over the short, prickly grasses and bushes, around the piles of snow wall boulders. In the steep rock channels below, waves thundered onto the jagged edges of the cliffs. The horizon remained clear of pursuers.

Teta had finished reciting the story of Isma for the third time. She raised the branch to the sky and shouted with all the energy of one who has successfully completed a long and difficult task, only to find how enjoyable the challenge had been.

This is the story of the first tooth. This is the story of Isma. I send heartfelt thanks to Isma for her story.

Her feelings of joy died as her stomach twisted in shock. A heavy fog clung to the opening of the rock channel. Soon the entire coast would be shrouded in the deadly covering.

Teta shoved the branch into Moonhead's hands. He, too, stood staring, no doubt wondering how he could have let this creep up on them without noticing.

"Come," Teta cried, retracing their steps back toward a pile of stones that seemed to hover in the swirling greyness.

"See, this is my father's Three Sun Cairn. I think it looks like a man. All of them do," she chuckled. "The three spirals carved on the *arms* tell how many days walk we are from the South settlement. Whichever way the *nose* points is the direction you should travel to find shelter."

She moved toward the edge of the cliff. "This cairn has a very crooked nose. We have missed the second cave. It is down there." She waved her arm behind her and down to where the sea pounded itself into frothy surf.

"We won't have time to fish," she said as they scaled a steep, slippery natural ladder to the opening of a cave, "but Father usually leaves oil for a fire."

When Moonhead did not reply, Teta glanced up at him. She could just make out his tightly-clenched teeth. Their descent was causing his wounded side great pain.

Teta immediately started the fire, as much to keep out the fog as to provide light. To her relief she found some dried berries in a shell beside her sleeping corner. She shared these and the water from her pouch with Moonhead.

"You do not look well," she said as she pushed a strand of sweat-matted hair from his cheek. "Your side?"

Moonhead nodded and began to shrug out of his polar bear. Teta threw off her sealskin and knelt to look at Lome's bindings.

Firelight danced on his pale skin. Teta stared at her brown arms as she reached out to help Moonhead lie down. How fair he was, how smooth his skin, how pink.

She carefully removed the sealskin bindings. Some blood oozed from the upper edge.

"I know how to sew skins together, perhaps I should stitch..."

"No, Teta." Moonhead grabbed her arm. "No. I am not going to live much longer."

"Oh, Moonhead, you don't know that!" She felt the tears pricking her eyelids.

"Yes, I do know that, Teta." He bore into her soul with his cold blue eyes. "Soogat is near. I feel him. He will kill me, despite my being bonded to you, *because* I am bonded to you. Do not waste time sewing me together."

"The sea mist will cost us a half day's travel," she said,

swallowing against her rising fear of meeting Soogat. "At least I can bind you again and you might be more comfortable."

"I think I should tell you the next story while you do that," he said as he shifted his body to make her task easier.

"Yes," she replied, smiling at him. "I'm ready."

He held up the Branch of the Talking Teeth.

This is the story of the second tooth. This is the story of Shalag. Shalag was the niece of Isma.

Shalag grew up into a tall maiden with flowing golden hair and soon mated with Crahn. He took Shalag away from the land of the high mountains and the fast runners. He took her across a sea on tree branches laced together to an island that lay white in the sun.

Many dark-skinned people lived on this island where colourful birds nested in the trees. The island people said the birds' songs were messages from the land above the earth. Where there are birds, a safe hearth can be found.

Sharing this island were the squealers. They hid from the night's chill and sunned themselves in mid-afternoon. They lay under the trees and feasted on nuts and berries. These were no common berries. They were bigger than a man's fist and had juice that ran down the chins of those who ate them.

The squealers, so the people of the island believed, came from the land below the earth—the land of those who came before. They were said to possess the wisdom of the world. They could tell of life as it had been.

Shalag taught others how the two very different worlds could live together in harmony and balance. This, she said, was how the world should always be, and that humans should strive to achieve such a balance not only amongst themselves but with nature.

This is the story of the second tooth, the tooth of Shalag. I send heartfelt thanks to Shalag for her story.

He lowered the branch and shook it. Teta waited a few minutes before speaking.

"I have some questions. Can trees really bear berries as big as a man's fist? What are squealers and what colour were the birds?"

Moonhead's eyes crinkled in humour. "It is a story, Teta. You must add the finer points yourself. I know my uncle changed the descriptions of the birds depending on the age of his listeners. Squealers are like boars, only more used to man. I am sorry. Maybe... maybe if I was not running from Soogat, I could find better words." He shrugged, growing serious. "I am not trained as a storyteller."

"Maybe not," she said softly, placing her head on his shoulder as they lay close together, "but you tell lovely stories anyway."

"Now, listen to the story of Shalag two more times and then...," he cupped his hand around her shoulder.

"I know, Moonhead," she chuckled, "then I have to repeat it three times to you."

◆◆◆◆◆◆

The man-like cairn of stones rose up at Soogat out of the fog. He knew this would be a good place to camp. There would be no use travelling any farther, even though it was only high sun. He couldn't risk himself or any of his followers falling over the cliffs or getting separated from each other.

He let his fingers wander over the round stone, the cairn's head, and its bent, slanted nose. He cocked his head, studying the two swirls scraped onto the arms, and wondered what they

31

could mean, especially the spiral with what looked like a roof over it.

"We'll stop here," he said, rubbing his palm on the smooth head. "Not even Moonhead and Teta can travel through this."

Mukta and Aurtoo had insisted on coming with Soogat and the men. They were now helping to raise a circular tent which the two women had carried. For more a permanent campsite, a shallow interior pit was dug first, but not for this short stay.

Together, they bent the slight trunks of alder trees, tied them at a point in the middle, and attached small branches around to give support. When the animal skins had been draped over the structure and secured by a circle of stones, the travellers settled in.

Mukta did not join in the conversations, preferring instead to eat her dried meat in silence. Soogat left her alone. He felt sure she recognized this pile of rocks, but he refused to ask her.

Chapter Four

This is the story of the third tooth, the tooth of Beoth. I send heartfelt thanks to Beoth for his story.

Teta shook the Branch of the Talking Teeth and frowned at Moonhead. There were so many names to remember.

The sun had smiled wanly through the streaks of wind-swept mist, but only for a short time. Time enough, Teta recalled, for Moonhead to collect seaweed and limpets trapped in the rock pools and for her to snatch two eggs from a gull nesting near the cave entrance. She had taken only what was necessary and had praised the screaming gull for such generosity.

Now, as they pressed straight ahead for the nearest edge of the snow wall, Moonhead listened to her recitation of the story of the third tooth. That is, Teta frowned, with half an ear. Moonhead's attention was frequently turning to the horizon behind them.

Teta adjusted her neck rope of polished pebbles and tiny bird beaks and tugged at her sealskin. She could feel the air growing colder as they neared the Blue Water. Caribou herds were grazing, far from the vast forests that touched the boundaries of the Land of the South People. They found relief from biting insects when close to the snow wall.

"Again, for the third time," Moonhead prompted. "And remember, Beoth looked after herds of 'milk bellies'."

Teta fingered the third tooth. There was only one point jutting from the bumpy ridge. Moonhead had explained to her that whoever pulled the tooth from Beoth's head must have had difficulty. Sometimes the teeth were strongly attached to a jaw bone and had to be broken in order to get them out. Teta shivered at the thought.

This is the story of the third tooth. This is the story of Beoth.

Beoth, keeper of the Branch of the Talking Teeth, was a tall, red-haired man who made many journeys with his old father, Crahn. One day Beoth and Crahn found themselves in a beautiful, green valley with a mighty river flowing through it.

Many huts dotted the hillsides, away from harm when the winter snows melted and caused the river to overflow its banks. Down on those banks, where the grass grew thickest, grazed some animals that neither Beoth nor Crahn had ever seen before.

The valley people called them milk bellies and, by keeping them surrounded by stone walls, they didn't have to hunt any more. The milk bellies, in return for plenty of grass and fresh water, allowed the valley people to have their extra milk. When the milk bellies grew old, they were butchered for their tasty meat.

Beoth fell in love with Clo, a young girl with hair like the blackbird's wing. He decided to stay and Crahn travelled on. Clo's father, Arn, was keeper of the largest herd of milk bellies in the valley. He was happy to have a strong man like Beoth to take over caring for his herd.

One day an old herdsman came hurrying down the mountain to warn Beoth of a great rain. He said he had seen the terrible black clouds pouring their rain down on the mountains to the south. The old man asked permission to drive his milk bellies through Beoth's pasture in order to get his herd to safety faster. He told Beoth that he should also get his milk bellies out of their walled pasture and up to the safety of high ground.

However, Beoth did not believe the old man, who begged him to listen.

Beoth said he could see no dark clouds, and he would not move his milk bellies. He also refused him passage through.

The old man drove his milk bellies up the slope as far as he could, while Beoth laughed at his efforts. Beoth fell into a peaceful sleep and did not see the heavy clouds roll down on the valley. Nor did he hear the thunder as it hurled itself at the mountains.

When he awoke, he found himself drenched. Streams of water cascaded down the mountains and into the river, which was swelling into his walled pasture.

The milk bellies were very nervous. The bull mooaw trotted round and round, his huge horns narrowly missing Beoth who was trying to reach the in-out rock. The rain and rising river soon flooded the walled pasture. Young milk bellies were the first to fall under, then those who carried the unborn.

The bull grew frantic. Just as Beoth reached the in-out rock, which he intended to move to let the animals out, the bull pinned him on his sharp horns and crushed him against the wall.

Beoth had a son, named Cah, who knew about the Branch of the Talking Teeth and all its stories. He realized that his father's story would be about not listening to others who know better than you. It was Cah who dug the broken tooth out of Beoth's mouth.

This is the story of the third tooth, the tooth of Beoth. I send heartfelt praise to Beoth for his story.

"Very good, Teta," Moonhead said, patting her on the shoulder. Teta managed a small nod and handed him the branch. The teeth rattled as he tucked them under the white fur.

Snarling and a sharp yelping brought Teta to a halt. She shot out her arm to stop Moonhead. They froze. Ahead of them was a pack of great silver wolves feeding on a young deer.

Teta pulled Moonhead onto his stomach. He groaned softly. She motioned to him to keep quiet. She knew they were well within the wolves' scent and hoped that eating would keep them busy for a while. Perhaps the blood on their noses would cover the smell of approaching humans.

The slight roll of the land, she hoped, would keep them hidden as they crawled over the grassy lip of the sea cliff. If they crouched below the lip, on the gravelly underside, the wolves might pass by—unless they heard the slivers of grey-blue rock and tiny stones clattering to the sea.

The noise caught the attention of one wolf. Teta could not see the animal, but she could hear it sniffing the area. The wolf obviously sensed their presence. She held her breath until she thought the sound of her heartbeat would burst from her ears.

The wolf snarled and began trotting up and down the ridge. Twice it tried to dig at the sandy grass with sharp claws. Foiled, it stuck its head over the edge. Teta now saw the flaring nostrils and blood-stained, slobbering flesh of its mouth. Before long, the ridge was lined with wolves.

One frantic male jumped onto the shale alongside them and scratched ferociously to remain steady. Teta shrieked in terror.

Moonhead swung out with his walking stick. His feet, as they dug into the loose gravel, sent avalanches of stones down the slope. He struck the animal on the side of the head. It yelped in pain.

As Teta blinked in fear and relief, the huge silver wolf slid and then tumbled into the churning sea. The others howled and barked in anguish as the wolf's body disappeared.

Teta and Moonhead clung to their precarious perch—just

how long Teta wasn't sure, but the sun was touching the land before they had the courage to come out of hiding.

With aching, cramped legs and stiff, frozen fingers, Moonhead and Teta scrambled back over the ledge and lay exhausted on the rough grass. Long grey spikes of clouds poked at the sun's pink and orange rays. The sky was radiant with many colors, colors which would lessen as the sun set.

Moonhead reached for Teta's hand and squeezed it hard. She covered his long, pale fingers with her short, brown hand. For a time they sat there, fingers entwined, staring at the sea. Teta pushed the fear of Soogat from her mind and allowed herself to enjoy the moment.

"That was close," Moonhead said in a voice scratchy with emotion. "Lome has taught you well."

"Lome did not teach me to hide under the ridge," Teta chuckled. "I found that the underside of a cliff edge is the best place to hide from a father."

Moonhead's laughter whipped around them in the strong sea wind. Teta thought it was one of the nicest sounds she had ever heard. He grinned at her and she let her eyes wander over his face, enjoying the dimples at the one side of his mouth and the crinkles around his eyes. Seeing him happy was like lying in the sunny-side shelter of a snow wall boulder, warm and content. She had not experienced so intense a feeling before.

Soogat flashed into her mind's eye. Had it been only two winters since Soogat had trapped her in his father's hut, pinned her to the ground, and kissed her? She remembered struggling and crying out for help. She also remembered the hard slaps of his hand across her face, and Mukta's fury at her son's behaviour. Teta hoped Soogat had not behaved so roughly with any other girl.

Moonhead stopped smiling.

"You were thinking of Soogat, were you not?" he asked.

Teta groaned, for it was as though a cloud had passed over the sun.

"Do all your people look like you?" she asked, raising herself onto one elbow, suddenly sad when he withdrew his hand at her question.

Moonhead sat up, his knees tucked under his chin. His eyes took on an expression of sadness, of thinking back.

"No. Most of my mother's people have red hair, all shades of red hair, light and dark. Green eyes are as common as blue."

"Green?" Teta had only seen people with brown eyes, with the exception of Moonhead. "People have green eyes, like the lynx?"

Moonhead nodded.

"My father's people raided the land, called the Green Island, where my mother lived, and took the land and women for their own." Moonhead stretched out his legs and supported himself on his hands. "My father is from the Land of the Fjords. They are big, strong people with blue eyes and light-colored hair. There are some though who have black hair."

He pushed some hair behind one ear and then motioned to the beach in the distance.

"Our sand is yellow and sometimes white," he said. "I did not know there was such a thing as blue sand."

"When the sea rests and pulls away from the cliffs, the rocks along the shore glint blue rather than grey in the sun," Teta explained. "It's beautiful. That's why this is called the Land of the Blue Rock."

"Oh!" Moonhead nodded to show he understood.

"Is your mother waiting for you across the sea?" Teta asked, inching closer. Being near Moonhead gave her a tingling feeling in her stomach.

"No. No, she is not waiting," he said, suddenly very intent on a lichen-coated rock. "She died just before we set sail."

Teta pulled away. "Come on," she cried. She didn't want to talk about dead mothers. The absence of her own mother still made her ache inside. The fact that she and this strange, wonderful man shared such a loss caught at her heart.

"We should keep moving. We have some distance to go before we find the Four Sun Cairn." She jumped up and began running, turning slightly inland.

••••••

The wolves stood in a line, heads bent low, panting, yellow eyes inspecting the humans. Soogat and the others dared not move.

"Stare them down, Soogat," croaked Aurtoo.

"I might be able to stare down one wolf, old woman, but never a pack," Soogat said, trying not to move his lips.

With a series of sniffs the new lead wolf, a young, grey male, turned and walked across the tundra. The rest followed. Soogat breathed deeply to calm himself.

"They couldn't have been too hungry," said Mukta. "Of course, no smart wolf pack will attack a group of people armed with spear points and sharp sticks."

"No," Soogat replied, rubbing his hand down his face to release the tension, "but now that we know they are watching, we must keep closer together as we walk."

Soogat smiled at the retreating animals. He felt sure he was closing in on Moonhead. He would make Moonhead take him to Lome's cave, to Teta, before banishing him south to the Land of the Tree People.

He looked into the cloud streaked sky and prayed silently to the Goddess of All for success in his plan to attain his prize—Teta and the leadership of his people.

"Forgive me, my son, for interrupting your prayers," Mukta said, falling in to step at his side, "but I've had a thought. I believe it would be to your benefit to possess the Branch of the Talking Teeth."

"How?" he asked, slowing a little.

"There is power in the branch," she answered. "It is likely the people would be grateful if you were to return with it."

"You could be right, old mother. Thank you."

Soogat quickened his pace, making the rest of his party break into a run to catch up. He raised his eyes to the sky once more and added the Branch of the Talking Teeth to his requests.

◆◆◆◆◆◆

"I worry that you won't be able to keep all the tales straight in your mind, Teta," Moonhead said, a frown creasing his forehead.

"I'm trying," Teta retorted, feeling deeply hurt. "The names are so odd—all those strange creatures like fast runners and milk bellies and squealers. It's hard to find a place in my head for them when my eyes have never seen them."

"I know," Moonhead nodded.

"You've had years of listening," Teta said, straining her eyes against the deepening blue of approaching night, "yet you still can't recall all the details."

"Yes, I am sorry," Moonhead grasped her arm and they stopped walking. "I should be happy that you even want to learn. I am sure that Isma and the other storytellers would want me to pass on the tales to someone. I am very blessed to have been bonded to such a good student."

Teta caught his smile, but couldn't tell if his eyes were smiling, too.

"We'd better keep walking," she said. "Four Sun Cairn should be around here somewhere. The nose, when you are heading north, points to a resting hut for travellers." She moved forward. "If we miss the landmark, we'll end up in the bog."

Chapter Five

Lome's shelter of the Four Sun Cairn had always felt warm and comfortable whenever Teta and her father had rested there. This night was no exception.

Teta blinked against the smoke of the peat fire and gazed around her. Whoever had built this dwelling knew about cold winter nights and fierce winds. Her father had always denied any hand in its design. He merely added furs and renewed the supply of peat every year. The rest was exactly as he had found it many weather cycles before.

The shale walls, which were packed with mud and moss, made neither a circle nor a square. Bleached whale bone rafters formed a dome. Great clumps of prickly grass had been tied into bundles and then attached to the bones with many sinews. Thick caribou hides created a middle layer, fur-side in. The water-resistant pelts of beaver and seal provided protection from moisture. In the cycles of no sun, heavy snow was stacked around the hut and a tunnel dug for entry.

The floor was scooped out of the dirt and carpeted with moss which Lome changed every summer. Two flat-topped boulders flanking the fire invited the occupants to cook, or sit and think. Fur piles made luxurious beds. Teta pulled both her arms out from under her fur and clasped her hands behind her head.

As she surveyed the roof, her contented sigh filled the space around her. Along the length of whale bones swam Lome's carvings of whales, fish, and seals. A skull of a long-dead walrus hung at the meeting point of the rafters.

"I like this best of all my father's places," Teta said peacefully.

"Yes, it is good," Moonhead replied from his boulder seat. "I saw places like this on the terrible north islands when I travelled the sea with my father. The people there were shaggy, small people but very fine builders."

"Tomorrow we'll find a rabbit so that we may eat," Teta informed her companion, eager for the chance to demonstrate her hunting expertise. "I can almost taste it."

Moonhead nodded. His face looked drawn and pale, Teta thought.

"Do you want to tell me another story?" she asked, hoping to enliven him.

He shook his head. "No. I feel you have enough in your head for the moment."

Teta started to speak up about how little time there might be, but Moonhead raised his hand to silence her.

"Forgive me. I cannot think straight tonight," he stated. "I have no urge to speak or listen anymore."

"Then go to sleep, Moonhead. You must be tired," she answered, hoping he would pick up her genuine concern. "We'll be waking early."

"I cannot rest, at least not just yet," he sighed. "A hunted animal does not sleep."

✦✦✦✦✦

"Are we going to stop soon?" Aurtoo asked, barely able to keep the whine from her voice and her feet on the trail.

"No," barked Soogat.

"But it's time to rest and we had little to eat at high sun," she continued, shifting her load of the tent poles further up her sloping shoulders.

"I know that, old woman," Soogat shouted. His own weariness made him feel even more miserable. "We'll walk until I say stop. Chew on some dried meat from your pouch. And be quiet! Moonhead will hear you coming long before he sees you."

"He has nothing to fear from me," Aurtoo stated in her own defence.

"He would know you journeyed with me, Soogat, soon to be leader of the South People." Soogat smiled at the thought of Moonhead's discomfort.

"Don't let my son annoy you, old friend." Mukta stepped in beside Aurtoo. "Would you like me to tell you Moonhead's story of Bugt and where he went when he died? It might help you forget how tired you are."

"Oh, yes," Aurtoo said, clapping her hands.

"Sssh," Soogat threw over his shoulder. "I told you to be quiet. Remember the wolves are nearby."

Mukta cleared her throat and gathered her thoughts.

When the flesh and blood of the human body becomes weak with hunger, illness, injury, or old age, the spirit within that person grows restless. It longs for another body, but will not leave until the proper moment. It cannot journey to a new body until the old one is truly dead.

The spirit is also a kind and loving being that takes pride in putting the dying mind to rest; it shows the mind that all in not dark, evil or dangerous when death comes. The mind is given a chance to die in a vision of its choice, a dream. All people have their own vision of what is peaceful, happy, or restful.

When the mind has smiled and sighed in its dream, the spirit leaves gently, slowly, and journeys to another.

So said Moonhead to Bugt before he died.

"Mukta, old mother, come up here with me," Soogat whispered loudly. "I want to talk to you."

Mukta walked past the single file of men until she fell into step with her son.

"You make more noise shouting at us and shushing us up than old Aurtoo could ever make," Mukta said out of the corner of her mouth. "You could learn some compassion. Aurtoo is right. We should be in a camp circle by now. Your hatred for Moonhead is clouding your judgement."

"I want to know why Lome left the company of the South People yet never joined the North People," Soogat insisted.

"He had his reasons," Mukta replied in her much-used answer. She pulled her sealskin hood tighter over her cheeks. Soogat followed her example. The sea wind was cutting with brutal force.

"Old mother," Soogat said, shaking his head in exasperation, "that is no longer enough. When I am leader..."

"*If* you are made leader," she grunted.

"No, old mother, *when* I am leader of the South People," Soogat hissed through his teeth, "I must be the keeper of all the people's secrets. How else can I to act properly?"

Mukta's turned her head sharply. "Did you hear something, Soogat?"

"It's just the wind. Tell me about Lome. It is time!" Soogat swivelled his head to ease the growing tension in his neck and back.

45

"Listen! Something is coming," Mukta cried, scanning the greyness for movement.

"Tell me what I want to know," Soogat urged. "Then we shall stop."

"It was all because of Kaatka," Mukta said. She rubbed her hands up and down against her forearms.

Soogat was keenly aware of her nervousness; she was getting old and jumpy. He also knew that she was not really thinking about what she was saying. Her guard was down.

"Kaatka was the daughter of Plemukt, the leader of the North People," she continued in a quaking voice. "Many weather cycles ago Lome and Bugt both wanted her. She was beautiful. So there was a contest for her and Lome won. Bugt married me, Lome's sister. The two men used to sit across the fire and glare..."

Suddenly, screams rent the evening air. Soogat, Mukta, and the others spun around. In the dim light, Soogat could just make out the figures of three silver wolves bringing Aurtoo down. Stunned, he could think of nothing to do. His heart seemed to cease beating and his knees grew weak. Shoving him forward, Mukta pleaded with him to help her friend. Still, he could not make his limbs move.

For what felt like an eternity, he stared at the scene, his jaw hanging slack. Then he heard the crunching of bone and a gurgling. The noise churned in his guts and he thought he would be sick, disgrace himself in front of his men. This thought filled him with a new sense of panic and brought life back to his fear-locked body.

He yelled at the other men and rushed the wolves, slicing the air with his spear point and short blade. A yelp followed as one point met a target. The other two animals slinked off into the grey of the early night.

Soogat threw himself on the wounded wolf, digging his fingers into the animal's thick, greasy coat. His nostrils flared against the rancid stench of dried blood from past kills and those made more recently. How much of this blood belonged to Aurtoo?

With one strong arc, he viciously drove his short blade between the beast's ribs. The animal stopped struggling but Soogat did not let go until the mighty chest no longer moved. Once sure the animal was dead, he fell back onto the mossy ground.

Close by, Mukta knelt beside her friend and carefully removed the burden of tent poles. Soogat crawled over and slumped down beside his mother, expecting some praise.

"You should not have had to carry this," she whispered hoarsely, ignoring him completly. "I should have made my son stop long ago." Sobs rose in her chest.

Soogat reached out with shaking hands and by placing his fingers on Aurtoo's neck tried to stem the hot, sticky blood that ran from her throat. He knew that not even his mother could heal these wounds.

"I was trying to get some dried meat," Aurtoo whispered.

"Sssh, Aurtoo, sssh." Mukta cradled her friend's head in her lap.

"I am with my restless spirit." The words were so faint that Mukta and Soogat had to lean down to hear them. Aurtoo coughed and swallowed. "I will find my mind's dream...."

The head fell to one side, slipping from the protection of the sealskin hood.

Once more Soogat sense his mother's disappointment. Now Mutka would hold him responsible for her friend's death. She was right. He shouldn't have made Artoo carry the tent poles. He should have allowed them to rest. Then the old woman would not have been holding the meat that had attracted the wolves. He hadn't acted fast enough to prevent the hideous death of a respected elder.

In keeping with their custom, he stood up, lifted his arms to the Goddess of All, and prepared to make the sound of the animal he had killed. He formed his mouth into the shape of a wolf's muzzle and, half in respect for the animal's soul and half out of his own pain, he howled.

◆◆◆◆◆◆

Teta sat up and hugged her animal skins tighter. She turned her head to one side and strained to hear... what? Nothing. Just the howling wind, a wind that warned of coming ice.

In her sleep she had heard screaming, a woman screaming. Had she been dreaming? A shiver ran down the length of her spine. The shelter was dark behind the entrance covering of moose hide.

Teta reached for a slab of peat and jabbed the fire into greater life. When some small flames finally managed to chase the blackness away, Teta looked over at Moonhead.

He moaned, the branch clutched tightly to his chest. Teta breathed deeply in order to relax. Would Moonhead ever invite her to his side of the fire, she wondered? When would he smile at her the way the other young men had when she and Lome had lived with the South People or ventured to visit the North People?

The howling of a wolf splintered through the night silence. It sounded more like a man than a wolf. She shivered down into her furs.

Chapter Six

Teta's stomach grumbled about the water and grubs she had swallowed for breakfast before setting out. She was miserable and feeling annoyed with herself. Her short blade had missed that rabbit by a heartbeat and she hated grubs.

Moonhead had not eaten anything, and now he strode along without thought for her. He kept looking back, repeating that Soogat must be close.

More than once she fought down her sarcasm and an urge to shout that maybe they should have stayed in the shelter of the Four Sun Cairn, where they were warm and comfortable. Did he have to keep repeating that Soogat would kill him on sight? Couldn't he even try to defend himself?

Yet she knew that Moonhead stood a much better chance of survival among the North People, and she truly wanted Moonhead to live. She tugged on his sleeve and headed him toward the edge of the snow wall.

"Where did you get your stick?" she asked as she trotted alongside the walking stick, trying to match his pace. The early rays of the sun played tricks of light and shade over the swirls and curls in the carved wood.

"My grandmother."

The coldness in Moonhead's tone cut through her like an icy wind.

"Why don't you tell me your Beginning Story or your What Comes After Death Story?" Teta nudged him.

Moonhead, surly, would not meet her eyes. "You should ask

Mukta and Aurtoo to tell you. I made them up. They are not real stories."

"What?" Teta tripped over a grassy clump, a sign they were getting too close to the bog. She would have to guide Moonhead more toward the sea. "What does that mean? Not real stories?"

"It means they come from *my* head and I am not a storyteller, so they are not real stories." Moonhead spat the words at her in exasperation.

"I didn't know that only special people could tell stories," Teta said, feeling very confused. "I always thought that if a person had a tale to tell, they should tell it."

Moonhead drew in a deep breath as if trying to control his temper.

"When I was crossing the sea," he said, "I was alone, and afraid. I had a lot of time to think. I thought about what I saw—the endless water, the stars, the colored lights in the sky. I thought about what might happen to me. Death, like my father, uncle, and brother." He shook his head. "Perhaps I had some sickness. The ideas became stories which I said over and over to myself. So, when they seemed to make Bugt and Aurtoo happy, I used them."

Teta drew her brows together and scanned the horizon. Salt air and the smell of the sea combined in her nostrils. Ice mountains sliced the grey water. There was no sign of Soogat.

"I do not understand the difference between your not-real stories and those on the Branch of the Talking Teeth," she admitted, hoping he would not become angry.

"The stories on the branch are very old and teach us lessons about ourselves," Moonhead answered with emphasis. "Mine are only the ramblings of a sick and frightened boy."

"Oh," said Teta, quite at a loss about how to continue. Gulls screeched in the blue sky above. A small herd of caribou, led by a bull with huge antlers, sauntered past on their way inland. Teta hoped the bull knew where the bog ended.

"I've been thinking about many things, too," she sighed, neatly sidestepping some newly-deposited, steaming caribou dung.

"Just what have you been thinking about?" Moonhead cocked his head and smiled a patient smile, though his eyes scanned the distance.

"Well, I've often wondered why both the sun and moon are bright in the sky, yet shed different light, and why the moon doesn't give off any heat," she replied, not looking at Moonhead in case he was laughing at her. "Or why the hairy beasts no longer live. Or how a person's eyes betray how they are feeling?"

"So?" He poked her with his elbow. "Have you found any answers? Are you creating your own stories?"

"The thoughts chase each other about in my mind," she shrugged and shook her head, "but the words have not come into my mouth yet."

"They will, Teta. They will because you are special." Moonhead gazed up into the sky and she knew he had not taken her lightly.

"What happened to your boat, what did my father call it... the kuruko?" she questioned, watching the way the wind whipped the lank strips of his white hair from side to side.

"Soogat convinced Bugt to light it and set it out to sea." Moonhead's lips tightened. "I tried to stop them, but Soogat said it would be the only way to keep me with the South People. Bugt agreed." He paused and glanced back over his shoulder.

Teta shook her head. "That must have made you very sad."

"Yes," he spoke softly. "I knew then that I would never be returning to my homeland."

"So the settlement of the South People became your home," Teta countered. "I heard you were at Mukta's fire and that she took good care of your needs."

"She was good to me," he nodded, "but Soogat lived there, too, and that was not always so good."

"Were you unhappy?" she asked, wishing he had sought her father sooner. He would have been happy with them.

"There was laughter," he admitted, "and great kindness."

"Mukta told us that you were the best person she had ever met," Teta confided, mesmerized by the way his face moved as it changed expressions. "She told us that you were fair to others and you understood people."

"Stop," he said sharply. "I did the best I could to survive. I found that being gentle and sensible and listening to others' problems helped them to accept me better."

"I didn't mean that being kind and understanding made you weak," Teta cried, suddenly wishing she could start the day over again.

"The women of the South People are intelligent and give good advice," Moonhead stated. "Yet those same women are often attracted to those men who are strongest, loudest, and most reckless."

"Yes, so I've been told by my father." Teta sighed. "Is it not the same everywhere?"

"So it seems. Now I will tell you the next story on the branch," Moonhead said, pounding the earth with his walking stick on every fourth pace. He removed the branch from under the polar bear fur and shook it at the wind.

This is the story of the fourth tooth. This is the tooth of Cah.

Cah had become a mighty warrior. In the land where he travelled, he had no choice. He had to kill or be killed. Despite the teaching of the tooth of Isma, he learned to fight.

In a short time, Cah was made leader of the People of the White Sea Rock, a fierce and tireless people. Many journeys were made into the nearby settlements, where Cah and his men would steal animals...

"Stop," Teta cried. "They stole animals? How can a human steal an animal? They roam wild in the forests, or on the grasses, or they swim in the sea."

"These people are like the keepers of the milk bellies. They put the animals behind walls or... lines of cut down trees. Please, just let me finish before asking any more questions," Moonhead pleaded.

Many journeys were made into the nearby settlements, where Cah and his men would steal the animals.

One of the problems the people in this part of the world faced was fog. It was so thick that men got lost out in the moors and bogs.

Cah had his men on a stealing journey when a dense fog caught them off guard. The men grew frightened and started to argue amongst themselves. Cah knew he had to keep them calm or they would begin fighting with each other; or they might wander off and die in the bogs.

Cah did two things. He made all the men tie themselves to each other by using their belt ropes. That way not even the weakest or most frightened could stray.

The other thing he did was recite the stories of the Branch of the Talking Teeth. This he did over and over. He soothed the minds of his men and passed the time until the fog blew away in the morning sun.

He learned that when you have lost your way, be patient. A path will reveal itself in time. He also learned that when you are deeply troubled, lean on those things that have always given you comfort. Your troubles will eventually fade.

Cah left the People of the White Sea Rock soon after, and with him travelled with his granddaughter, Mo'aq, to whom he passed the branch.

This is the story of the fourth tooth, the tooth of Cah. I send heartfelt thanks to Cah for his story.

Teta gazed up into Moonhead's serious blue eyes. "I'll always remember that story," she said. "Every time we have fog, I will remember it."

He gave a little snort. "Good. Now listen again."

Teta felt that the repetition was unnecessary. This was a story she'd had experience with. Her thoughts drifted across the rocky shore and into the sky with the puffins. When her turn came to recite the story of Cah, she took the branch, shook it at the wind, and did not make one mistake.

She wondered about putting milk bellies and other animals behind stone walls. How would a great cat manage behind a line of broken trees? He would jump over or crawl through. How would a man, even a fierce warrior like Cah, steal a great cat?

Teta decided this was another one of those pieces of interesting information she did not understand. Stealing a great cat would make a good story.

"Does the branch need any special care?" she wondered aloud, noticing that Moonhead's nose had grown red from the cold wind.

"I do not know," he said, turning the wood over in his hand. Teta caught the remorse in his voice. "I should have paid more attention when I sat on my grandmother's knee."

"Your grandmother?" Would she ever work her way through his relatives? "I thought your uncle was the storyteller?"

55

"He was." Moonhead's face darkened. He scowled down at the ground. "My grandmother told my uncle the stories. Grandmother's name was Mo'ag."

"Ah," Teta laughed. "Mo'ag was Cah's granddaughter. She gave you the walking stick. You see I am paying attention." She clapped her hands. "Tell me Mo'ag's story, please."

"I just finished telling you one story," he poked at the tooth of Cah. "Do you feel ready for another? He fingered the tooth of Mo'ag.

"Yes," she laughed again, poking the tooth of Cah, her eyes sparkling. "I'm ready." She fingered the tooth of Mo'ag, the fifth tooth, enjoying the lightheartedness of the moment.

"After that I will not tell you another until night," he said with authority. "Your head will become too full."

She shrugged and tried hard to send him her most alluring smile. She knew she had slipped through his protective skin by the way he grinned back.

This is the story of the fifth tooth. This is the story of Mo'ag.

Mo'ag had long hair the colour of honey, but her face was very plain. She was, however, a highly respected member of her settlement.

Her husband was chieftain of the People of the Rainbow Fish River. The land around the river was hilly and the air was damp and cold. The people survived because of the Rainbow Fish River. When the large salmon hurled themselves against the strong river, the People stood in the middle or along the banks and caught these fish with their hands.

Mo'ag, more than any other settlement person, loved the salmon. She would sit watching them, tickling them as they rested in the quiet pools, shining a fire branch near the water so the fish would surface.

One rainy day a stranger came upon Mo'ag lying on her stomach, watching the fish. He went near her thinking that this lady with the lovely hair would also have a lovely face to match. He barely hid his disappointment when Mo'ag turned to greet him. He went away without talking to her further.

Later, another stranger came by while Mo'ag watched the salmon. The second stranger admired Mo'ag's hair and expected to see a great beauty. He, too, turned from her without speaking after she looked up at him.

Just before darkness fell, a third stranger saw Mo'ag lying by the stream. He noticed the honey-coloured hair, but he also noticed the faces of the fish above the water level. Their mouths were opening and closing as if talking.

He was so struck by the sight that he approached Mo'ag. When she turned he did not leave, but instead smiled and asked her how she got the fish to come so close. She spoke with this man for a long time.

In the sky a rainbow appeared and in the man's heart a new understanding grew. When he looked at the woman he saw beautiful hair but a plain face. When he looked into her eyes, into her heart, he saw great beauty and wisdom.

Mo'ag brought the stranger to her chieftain husband and told him about the two other men. The chieftain rewarded the man's curiosity and willingness to learn by giving him one of his daughters and some land beside the river.

But Mo'ag rewarded him with her friendship and from then on, the stranger and Mo'ag taught the people to look for beauty in the heart, to live in harmony with all creatures, and to work hard at a task until you have mastered it.

This is the story of the fifth tooth, the tooth of Mo'ag. I send heartfelt thanks to Mo'ag for her story.

"Hmn," Teta said softly. "I feel I know the story. My father has tried to teach me such things. He will like this story." Then her mind made a thought connection. "And your uncle, the storyteller, was the son of Mo'ag's daughter and the stranger."

Moonhead nodded, shook the Branch of the Talking Teeth at the wind, and repeated the story of his grandmother, Mo'ag.

The sun was at high time when they came upon two seagulls pecking at a puffin. The courageous bird fought and struggled but was quickly running out of strength.

Moonhead sat cross-legged, not far from the flying feathers, beckoned Teta to join him, and waited. Before long, the puffin stopped struggling.

Moonhead jumped to his feet and swung his walking stick at the surprised gulls. He picked up the dead bird and brought it to Teta.

"Hungry?" he asked softly, looking very amused.

Teta nodded and grinned back.

◆◆◆◆◆◆

Soogat yawned, stretched, and rubbed his belly. He still felt satisfied by the hearty meal of wolf from the night before. The remains of the animal had provided a fine fire when added to the moss.

The silver hide lay stretched out in front of him. He rolled it and strapped it onto the bundles of one of his men. The tent and the leftover meat had been packed up and distributed among them for easier carrying.

They had dug an indentation into the earth for Aurtoo's body and covered it with small rocks. Perhaps, Soogat grinned into the morning wind, when they returned to the South People, he could blame Moonhead for the old woman's death.

He climbed onto one of the large boulders left by the snow wall and scoured the distance for signs of Moonhead. Caribou grazed lazily nearby and rabbits darted between their knobby legs.

Sea birds flocked along the jagged cliffs, their calls loud and energetic, but he could still hear the sea. Soogat found the travel north exciting. Until now, he had only travelled south, to the forests and rivers of his grandmother's people. Since long ago, the North People were noted for their unfriendly attitude toward the South People. The trouble over Kaatka had only worsened things.

He turned slightly and was just about to jump down when a far off movement caught his eye. Two tiny figures on the horizon were moving rapidly toward the edge of the river.

Two people, travelling together. One, obvious in the great snow bear, was Moonhead. The other, smaller, slighter, bouncing around like a lynx kitten, black hair flying behind, could only be—Teta!

Soogat gasped as the harsh hand of jealousy grabbed his heart. Teta and Moonhead! Lome had allowed Teta to journey with Moonhead, and by the way Teta was skipping and gesturing, she was happy to be going.

Another hand, this time the hand of anger, threatened to stop Soogat's heart from beating altogether. How could the old man do something as irresponsible as sending Teta off into the wild lands with no protection other than Moonhead? Moonhead was wounded and being chased, his very life at stake.

Then the figures disappeared.

Soogat gave a short cry and leapt off the boulder. He yelled at his companions to start moving because he could see Teta and Moonhead on the horizon. His men laughed and started off immediately. Each one slapped him on the back and gave words of praise and encouragement.

"He has my Teta," he cried loudly, breaking into a run. "If he has so much as smiled at her I will bury him deep, with his face to the ground. All of you, mark my words."

As he passed Mukta, she stared at him in stony silence. This vendetta had cost her friend's life. She had not spoken to him since the wolf's attack, and he did not know when, or if, she would ever speak to him again.

✦✦✦✦✦✦

"My father told me to turn inland when we came to the delta," Teta explained, slipping her hand into Moonhead's free one and leading him away from the sea. "He said the streams are narrower and easier to cross. He also said that when we reached the river delta, the land would be lower. If Soogat is following us, he will not be able to see us until he is also near the rivers."

"I wanted to watch the waterfalls," Moonhead shouted.

Over the edge of the black-blue cliffs tumbled torrents of water, not at just one outlet but many. The Blue Water Rivers cascaded into froth where they met the churning ocean.

Even as Moonhead stared at the rivers, Teta sensed his heart was heavy. To break the tension, she chattered on about the shapes and colours of the river pebbles. Now and then she stopped and chose a stone of exquisite design or colour and dropped it into her pouch.

"This one I will polish until it shines like the sun," she cried excitedly, moving the little rock around in the palm of her hand. Then she grew solemn and started peering into the shallow ripples.

"Ah, ha! Here." She straightened and waved Moonhead over to where she stood on a large flat rock at the edge of a river. "Now I have another the same. I'll start a new neck rope with these pebbles. I'll call them the Moonhead Stones because they remind me of your eyes."

Moonhead gazed down at the pale blue stones. The look on his face betrayed the extent of his loneliness.

"Tell me the last legend," she whispered, forcing him to meet her eyes.

"This is a difficult story for me," he admitted. "I must tell the story of my uncle for the very first time. I have been trying to hear it in my head." He stopped and shook the branch again.

"This is the story of the sixth tooth. This is the story of Labhradair.

Labhradair was a great storyteller. His very name meant 'speaker.' He could tell all the stories on the branch in all their glory. He was much loved by the people of the Green Island.

Labhradair, as with other storytellers, liked to travel. In the company of his sister's man, Galeif, and Galeif's sons Cuimhne, the elder, and Mearanach, the younger, Labhradair started on the long voyage.

The wind blew with enough force to carry the kuruko well on the way to the Island of Ice. Galeif was an experienced man of the sea and sail, and he had taught his sons all he knew.

After several nights, land finally came into view, and they went ashore the Island of Ice. They filled their water bags, hunted some birds and fish, then took some time to look around.

The Island of Ice was a barren, dismal place. A great mountain of smoke rumbled continuously. Galeif seemed not to worry, but Labhradair was anxious and insisted upon leaving before it was too late. He said that he could read the signs in the sky. He said over and over that nothing good would come of their staying longer.

Galeif finally agreed to set sail one morning when the roaring of the mountain had grown very loud. Smoke billowed from the opening and the earth shook. They managed to get off the Island of Ice, but whatever had caused the mountain to erupt made a terrible sea tide. It swept Labhradair and the others in the opposite direction far from the Green Island. Labhradair grew frantic.

They sailed, carried by the strange wind and angry sea, for the same amount of time as they had from the Green Island to the Island of Ice. From out of the horizon one twilight came a coastline, a coastline so hazy Galeif thought he imagined it.

Without difficulty they landed on a pebbly beach. Although the strip of land near the sea was green and full of colourful wild flowers, all they could see in the distance was snow and ice.

On this land, which Labhradair named Sneachda Land, Galeif fell ill. His breaths came in short, raspy sounds and sweat broke out on his forehead. Labhradair, acting on Galeif's instructions, sailed back out to sea.

Galeif grew weaker and weaker. His skin grew hot and his eyes glazed over. His chest rumbled with every breath. Not long after they left Sneachda Land, Galeif died. His body was thrown out of the boat and into the dark grey swells of the cold sea. His passing lay heavily on the minds and hearts of those left on the kuruko. Mearanach wept long into the dark time.

Soon after, Labhradair collapsed onto the floor of the kuruko. He, too, seemed to suffer from that which had killed Galeif. Before he fell into the heavy sleep, Labhradair called Cuimhne to him and handed him the Branch of the Talking Teeth.

Cuimhne was training to be the next storyteller. Cuimhne knew how to look after the branch, how to tell the tales with detail and colour. Before Labhradair died, Cuimhne stated that Labhradair's story would be about the importance of paying attention to nature's signs and your inner voice. If Galeif had heeded Labhradair's warnings, neither would have fallen sick. They would have returned safely home to the harbours of the Green Island.

Then Labhradair, the great speaker, breathed his last.

This is the story of the sixth tooth, the tooth of Labhradair. I give heartfelt praise to Labhradair for his story.

Teta stared up at him in silence. She could feel his panic. His parents and brother were dead. His boat lay charred and ruined. He believed his life was nearing its end.

Teta willed her kindness and warmth, which he had kept at a distance, to flood over him like the Blue Water River flooded over the cliffs. To her surprise, he reached out and roughly wrapped her in his arms.

Teta hugged back as tightly as she could without losing either her balance or the Moonhead Stones. His acceptance of her, at last, filled her heart with warmth. Slowly and awkwardly, he released her.

"Come. We must move on," he said, his eyes sweeping the land.

"I will fill the water skins here," Teta replied in as matter-of-fact a tone as she could muster.

He walked a little ahead of her as she adjusted the skins over her shoulder. Had he always been so tall? Had the sun always covered his hair with such golden light?

She sighed. They would not reach the next cairn, with its pointed slate nose and curled lines indicating a waterfall, until night. Although the Waterfall Cave was not far, they would need to hunt for food and gather fuel. Lome had warned Teta that since the People of the North often used Waterfall Cave, he could not guarantee any provisions would be there for them.

Tonight, she decided, as she caught up and once again matched Moonhead stride for stride, she would lie with him on the same side of the fire.

Chapter Seven

Dampness coated Waterfall Cave, which smelled of fish and mold. Still, Teta knew Soogat would never find them down here, just beyond the cliff edge and under the largest Blue Water stream's drop to the sea. Only someone who knew how to interpret the Waterfall Cairn could ever locate the cave.

Moonhead, while searching the cliffs above for signs of Soogat, had speared a seal. They had enjoyed the meal immensely, but talk had been scarce because of the thunderous noise made by the tumbling water.

The cave was very cold. Soon, ice would form on the handholds and the climb behind the waterfall would be impossible.

Teta knelt on the floor smoothing their furs. The polar bear would serve as their covering. She looked at Moonhead who sat cross-legged on a cushion of gathered moss. He seemed to be watching her in a way that made her happy and yet nervous.

"It's damp in here," she said, smiling through lips that quivered with cold.

In one fluid movement he lay in front of her, one hand extended in bidding. She let her fingertips linger in the warm, dry palm before lying on her stomach beside him. He drew the polar bear over them and took a deep breath. Teta could feel the air from his nostrils on her cheek and the welcomed heat of his body next to hers.

The Branch of the Talking Teeth rattled as Moonhead shook it at the ceiling of the dark cave.

"Now I shall try to tell you the rest of the story up to the part where I am saved by Soogat," he said.

"Is this to be the legend of the seventh tooth, the legend of Mearanach, Moonhead?" Teta asked, barely able to contain her excitement.

"I am not worthy of a place on the branch," he sighed, placing the branch on the floor near his head. "I am just telling you how I got to your land. Listen, so you may better understand."

"I will listen, Moonhead," she replied solemnly.

He gathered in his breath and began.

"I could not bring myself to watch my brother dig into Labhradair's gums for the next tooth. I did, however, cut and braid the lengths of Labhrahair's hair into a string to attach the cleaned tooth to the branch.

"Cuimhne raised the branch to the sea wind and shook it. We spent the next night retelling the stories of the Branch of the Talking Teeth and, with the sun's first rays, threw Labhradair's stiffening body into the sea.

"We drifted and rocked on the water. Storms tried to turn the vessel upside down, but Galeif had built it specifically for the long voyage. Water and food grew scarce.

"I started to shiver and shake during one terrible storm. I covered myself in fur skins, and fell asleep deep under the covered portion at the back of the kuruko.

"How long I slept, I do not know. When I opened my eyes, I was stiff and sore, my throat was dry, and my chest hurt to breathe. I called for Cuimhne but he did not answer me.

"I crawled around looking for him, calling his name, but Cuimhne was not anywhere on the boat.

"I pulled myself up to look over the side of the boat but could see nothing, no floating body, no clothing, no Cuimhne. Had the storm-tossed boat thrown him into the sea? I threw myself down onto the floor of the kuruko and began screaming. I pounded my fists on the floor, hitting my left hand on something that rattled.

"Cuimhne had left behind the Branch of the Talking Teeth."

Moonhead sniffed and picked up the branch.

Teta reached her hand across his naked belly, careful not to touch his wounded side, and held him tenderly as he wept.

◆◆◆◆◆◆

"Where have they gone?" Soogat snarled through his clenched teeth. He stood on two flat stones in the middle of one of the Blue Water Rivers and squinted at the far bank. The sun dipped into the land, sending lengths of orange and yellow into the pale grey sky.

Mukta and the men were raising the tent. Her eyes kept straying to the cairn. Soogat stomped over and walked around it. He touched the stones, poking at the ones which stuck out. He was particularly interested in the thin, sharp piece of slate with the engraved spirals and squiggles that pointed to the sea.

He marched back to the waterfall and lifted his nose to smell the wind. He wondered if Teta had found any fuel to light a fire and cook some food. If so, he might be able to detect the smoke.

He paced back and forth at the river's edge, then went back to the camp. He stopped in front of his mother and lifted one eyebrow. He waited for her to answer his unspoken question, to help him benefit from her knowledge of the Land of the North People, to tell him if she knew anything about these cairns.

Mukta raised her own eyebrow, turned her back on him, and walked to the Blue Water River to fill the water skins.

◆◆◆◆◆◆

Teta could see the moon was shining, even through the veil of water. She would have dearly loved to take Moonhead down to the sea's edge and sit where they could watch the shimmering waves together.

Moonhead had stopped crying a short while ago, but she kept her own counsel. She knew it would be best for him to speak first, when he was ready.

"Teta." She could hear his voice throbbing through his pounding heart as her head lay on his chest. "I must thank you again for being willing to learn the stories. You are a good listener and I think you will make a fine storyteller."

She wriggled closer instead of answering.

"After Soogat kills me...," he started.

"Don't say that," she cried, raising her face to his in the darkness.

"Teta, Soogat will kill me," Moonhead argued, patting her shoulder. "So, after he does, what will you do? I can only hope he does not harm you or Lome."

"I'm not afraid of Soogat, neither is Lome," Teta stated strongly, feeling invincible in the depths of the Waterfall Cave.

"You should be. He is very angry." Moonhead stroked her

hair as it lay down her back. "When he finds out you are bonded to me, he will be even angrier, if that is possible."

"The first thing I'll do *if* he kills you," she replied, tracing his throat with her fingernail, "is pull out one of your teeth, cut some of your hair, and attach the seventh tooth, the tooth of Mearanach, to the Branch of the Talking Teeth."

She felt Moonhead's body tense, and when he spoke his voice sounded veiled. "I am not worthy of a place on the branch."

"You are worthy, Moonhead. You have told me all the stories that were taught to you," Teta said, moving her body until their heads were equal. "You voyaged across the sea and lived while the others did not. You won the hearts of a people who are very different from you." She touched his cheek with her palm. It was cool and smooth. "You brought peace with stories which you, yourself, made up in your own head. You possess the branch. I say you are worthy, and I will dig out your tooth."

She could tell he thought about her words by the silence that followed. She ran her finger around his nose and eyebrows. He caught her hand and kissed it lightly.

"Hmn. I can only hope you are right. Be sure to ask Mukta and Aurtoo about the stories I made up," he whispered, rolling onto his side to face her. The movement caused her to fall onto her back. "I do not wish to talk any further to my mate. I have a better way to pass the night."

✦✦✦✦✦✦

Soogat pretended to be asleep as Mukta sat at the door of the tent. He watched while the stars surrounded the moon and then faded into the pale grey streaks of morning.

69

Judging from his mother's actions, Moonhead and Teta were close. She knew a lot more than she was letting on. Soogat snored back a growl. He would earn her admiration once he had shown Moonhead mercy and embraced Teta as his own. Then, as leader, he would be respected—by everyone.

He shifted slightly and pulled his furs over his ears. Mukta turned to him at the movement. Quickly, he shut his eyes again and let his lips smack together. She went back to searching the dawn.

He frowned. A vision of Teta and Moonhead together—eating, talking, laughing. Oh, Goddess of All, the hurt of that thought! Then a greater pain shot through his soul as an unwanted image pierced his mind. Moonhead and Teta wrapped in each other's arms.

He began to shake. Curling his body tightly into a ball, he prayed, silently.

"Oh, Goddess of All, not that. Oh please, not that. I do not know what I would do."

He heard Mutka heave a series of heavy sighs. He was close, very close. Mukta's restlessness proved it.

In the dim recesses of the tent, Soogat opened one eye and smirked at his mother's back.

Chapter Eight

A drizzle covered the coastline. Teta stood on the ledge to the right of the waterfall and gazed at the moisture dripping from the handholds. She reached for the first one and fit her fingers into the rough opening. Slippery rock warned her against trying the climb.

Moonhead came up behind her and draped her fur skin over her shoulders.

"Rain," he said, and cursed.

Teta could barely conceal her own annoyance.

"This isn't good. The handholds are very wet. We could fall and..."

"And what," Moonhead smiled wryly. "Die? You stay here. I can find my way to the North People if you give me directions. There is no need for you to put your life in any more danger than it already is. I will die soon anyway."

"Stop," she cried, stamping her foot. "I don't want to think about that. If you go, then I go."

"Then, let us go." Moonhead pushed his walking stick through his leather belt, placed his fingers carefully in the handholds, and stretched his foot into the first step. "I do not think this weather will slow Soogat down at all."

Teta bit her lip. The thought of losing Moonhead now that they were finally growing closer, now that they had shared more than just stories and food, left her weak inside.

She took a quick look down into the froth where the waterfall collided with the surf. Seals barked on the rocks. Puffins, gulls, and gannets vied for the fish just below the water's surface.

The drizzle gathered on her fur skin and at the ends of her hair like sparkling points of light. She took a deep breath and started out after Moonhead.

Once, he lost his footing and hung by his fingertips. Teta guided his toes to the nearest step. He grunted in thanks and continued on. The climb was slow and tiring. Finally they pulled themselves onto the level ground and lay side by side, panting.

The thwack of a spear point piercing the ground between them made Moonhead and Teta spring to their feet. Her heart skipped a beat when she found herself face to face with Soogat.

Soogat glared at Moonhead. Teta heard Moonhead swallow. She was proud of the way he did not drop his eyes from those of his hunter.

"Moonhead! Teta?" came a distant, anxious voice.

Teta stole a quick glance over Soogat's shoulder to where, outside a tent in the distance, Mukta was being held by two men. Another stood directly behind Soogat, the excitement evident on his dirty face.

"My old mother is worried about you, Moonhead." Soogat's tone sent shivers through Teta's already cold body. "When she saw you come over the cliffs, she tried to warn you, but I was ready."

He shot Teta an icy look when Moonhead remained silent.

"You will answer to me later!"

Teta bristled. "I don't have to answer to you, not ever."

"Leave her alone." Moonhead's words rode clearly over the gulls and pounding waterfall. "Your argument is with me."

"There's no argument," Soogat snapped, sticking his face

close to Moonhead's. Teta could see their breath, steaming in the chill air, the moisture dripping from Soogat's nose. "You've managed to strip me of my rightful place as leader of the South People."

"You are not leader yet," Moonhead replied.

"Because you turned my people against me with your stories and your strange ways." Soogat spat on the grass. "I despise you."

"I did not turn your people against you," Moonhead snorted. "You have done nothing to win them over." He paused and one corner of his mouth twisted in a wry smile. "I owe my life to you. I wanted only to be your friend."

"Hah!" Soogat exploded in a mirthless sound. "Do friends make you feel worthless and unwanted by your own people? Do friends spend the night with your pledged mate?"

"I am not your pledged mate," Teta shouted back, moving between the two men.

"Teta, no! Keep silent!" Moonhead warned, grabbing her by the arms and moving her aside.

"What?" Soogat's burning eyes swivelled from Teta to Moonhead and back to Teta. "What do you mean, you're not my pledged mate? Kaatka and Mukta made the pledge when I was two summers old and you were born in that early spring. You know that."

"I am bonded with Moonhead." As soon as the words left her mouth, Teta wished she could cut out her tongue. She glued her eyes to Moonhead's profile, knowing that Soogat stared at her.

For a moment, no one moved. Even the gulls did not fly overhead.

A low growl in Soogat's throat alerted Moonhead. He had just enough time to pull out his walking stick and jump away from the cliff edge.

Soogat dove after him and the force of his effort brought them both down upon the wet earth. Moonhead and Soogat rolled over and over, arms and legs locked in combat.

Teta tried tearing them apart, but Soogat's man pulled her off and gripped her firmly. Her stomach turned over and she thought she would be sick.

Soogat got to his feet and raised his short point. Teta screamed as Moonhead managed to scramble away from the plunging blade. Green streaks from the wet grass soiled the polar bear fur.

"Fight, Moonhead." Teta struggled against her captor. "Fight."

As Soogat charged, Moonhead swung his stick. With a dull whump the wood struck Soogat across the side of his head. He howled and reeled back a couple of steps.

He approached Moonhead again and this time the stick caught him in the small of the back as Moonhead danced around him. Soogat screamed in pain and anger.

Soogat tackled Moonhead at the knees, forcing the stick to fly out of his hand. Soogat felt the power of Moonhead's fists in his stomach and face. He scrambled to his feet and kicked whatever he could reach—ribs, head, groin.

Once more the polar bear fur was dragged through the mud. This time when Soogat raised his blade, Moonhead did not escape. The blade sliced through the air, through the white bear skin, and into Moonhead's chest. Teta screamed and sank to the ground. Again and again, Soogat drove the short point into his enemy until the great bear fur was stained red with blood.

Teta knelt forward and vomited. "Moonhead," she groaned.

Soogat got to his feet, exhausted. He blinked and ran his hands across his brow to wipe away the wetness of his sweat and the rain. He stared at the bloodied body, the pale, dead face. A shudder snaked down his body. He had killed Moonhead!

He took a deep breath. An unusual silence lay on the land. For a moment even the wind rested.

He had killed the storyteller.

"Moonhead," he cried, his voice so full of emotion that Teta was forced to look up. For a brief moment, Teta thought she saw sadness instead of exultation.

But then Soogat picked up the walking stick. He turned to the tent in the distance, raised his fists, and bellowed in triumph.

Teta stumbled over the slippery earth to Moonhead's side and cradled his head in her lap. Despite his efforts, he had been no match for Soogat. He had not even drawn his short point.

While Soogat accepted the praise of his men, Teta reached under the polar bear covering and removed the Branch of the Talking Teeth. She slid it under her own fur skin. Somehow she would have to get a tooth and soon, before the jaw stiffened in death.

But for now, tears blinded her and her sobs mingled with the renewed cries of the sea birds.

✦✦✦✦✦✦

"Teta, dear Teta," pleaded Soogat. "The day is over. Nighttime draws near. Please let my men wrap Moonhead in hides so we can carry him more easily until we find a place for him. The rest of our people will meet up with us soon."

"You cannot have him," Teta cried. "I will not leave his side. I will sleep beside him and watch over him."

She truly wanted to stay near her Moonhead, but not only to grieve. She needed to get his tooth. The trudge back along the coastline to find a beach suitable for digging a grave would be gruelling and time-consuming.

Soogat hauled her to her feet. The action caused Moonhead's lifeless head to fall from her lap and stare at the stars. A cry of agony escaped from her lips.

Soogat shook her, none too gently. "He's dead. Come with me, now. Be a part of the living."

"No!" She swirled free. "I need to mourn him. I... I need to think."

"Think about what?" He poked her in the shoulder with his index finger. "About lying in his arms? About his pretty hair?" His prodding forced her to step backward.

"Have some pity, Soogat," she said dryly, pushing his hand away. "You're leader now. Don't be cruel." She would have liked to add "more than ever" but decided not to push him.

"The girl is right." Mukta's voice came out of the darkness. "She travelled with Moonhead. She deserves time to think about him before his body is removed from this world."

Soogat spun around. "So, old mother, you've broken your silence. Was it my bravery or my cunning that finally broke through?"

Mukta ignored his statements, chosing instead to stare out over the crashing waves.

"I've given the matter great thought," she said. "You've

conducted a fine chase, my son. But a mighty champion allows time for grief. Give the girl her time."

Mukta stood on her tiptoes and whispered in Soogat's ear. "She may be more willing for a pair of warm, strong arms if they belong to a kind heart. I know girls. Give her time."

Teta's throat tightened as she overheard her aunt's advice.

Soogat smiled at his mother and walked over to Teta.

"I am sad that you had to become involved in this, Teta," he said softly, touching her hair. "You may have tonight with your... with Moonhead."

He walked away toward the fire where his men were preparing pieces of the wolf meat.

Teta sank to the ground at Moonhead's side, between him and the light from the fire. Tears of her own pain burned under her eyelids. Mukta knelt beside her and patted her arm.

"How does he know that I won't run away?" Teta said bitingly, with an icy glance over her shoulder at Soogat's back.

Mukta snorted. "He is much too sure of himself. But he is also much too naive when it comes to understanding people's natures." She sat down with a grunt. "He's not a gentle man. It saddens me. However, I believe he might soften with age. Many men do."

"Thank you for helping me get some time with Moonhead." Teta gulped. She brushed her tears from her cheeks and tried to smile.

"Ach." Mukta flapped her hands. "I only told my son what he wanted to hear. It satisfied him."

Teta felt she could trust her aunt. They grinned at each other with understanding.

"I have the Branch of the Talking Teeth," Teta said in a conspiratorial voice.

"Good!" Mukta clapped her palms together. "I was wondering what became of it. Where is it?"

"In here." Teta patted her fur skin. "He told me all the stories while we were travelling. He gave me much of his people's ancient wisdom."

"I hope that was not all he gave you, girl," Mukta said, her eyes sparkling in the firelight.

Teta lowered her head. "He lay with me only once, old aunt, and that was last night."

"That is enough to produce a child," Mukta sighed contentedly.

Teta squinted at her. "Why does that please you? You should be angry that I've dishonoured my pledge to Soogat—your son."

Mukta winked. She grinned and her eyes became lost in wrinkles.

"I can see all this turning out well for everyone," she whispered. "Given time."

Teta would think more on Mukta's words later; she did not have the luxury of talking long now. There was a task to perform. She moved to Moonhead's shoulders. With shaking fingers, she pried open the jaw. Already, it had grown stiff.

"You need one of his teeth?" Mukta asked. "For the branch?"

Teta nodded, hating the feel of his cold skin of death. She stuck her finger in Moonhead's mouth and felt the ridges of his teeth.

"He didn't think of himself as a storyteller," she said.

"Ah, but he was." Mukta nodded her head. "Did he tell you his Beginning story and his After Death story?"

"No, he said you and Aurtoo would tell me those. We did not have much time together." Teta drew back. "How am I going to get the tooth out? My heart aches at the thought of hurting him even though he no longer feels."

Mukta reached under her coat and produced the stiletto point of a sharpened bird's beak.

"Here, use this," she said, and her words grew cold. "Aurtoo was attacked by a wolf. Her body lies back along the trail."

An anguished cry escaped from Teta as she accepted the pointed tool. The image of the great silver wolf tumbling into the surf leapt to her mind. But it was soon replaced by the memory of Aurtoo. Teta recalled many warm nights in the house of Aurtoo when the air had been filled with women's laughter. Words escaped her now, upon learning of such a useless death. She forced her mind back to the task at hand.

"Tell me the Beginning story," she said, softly, and turned the needle-sharp instrument around in her palm. Lovingly, she reopened Moonhead's mouth and peeked inside. She must appear to be preparing Moonhead for burial and couldn't make any suspicious moves. Mukta kept a wary eye toward the fire.

Mukta began Moonhead's story, her words quiet and soothing, her eyes alert. *In the beginning everything was dark and silent. The dark and silence grew and grew until it burst, causing a great shower of stars. Some of them are still falling and they can be seen now and then. One star was bigger than all the rest and pulsed with the potential to give life. We are living on that star.*

Teta stopped, amazed at what she heard. "Everyone knows the Great Mother created the world and all animals, flowers and everything. Even the sun and moon were created by the great spirits. The Goddess of All protects us."

She looked down at the open mouth, the pale moonlit face, and shivered. She knew so little about how Moonhead had thought. The long voyage must have sent him to the edge of madness. Such strange notions!

Teta chose a back tooth and ran the sharp point of the stiletto around it. She worked against her fear of Soogat discovering what she was doing and against her deepening grief. Teta tightened her hold on the tooth. The sounds of tugging and scraping tormented her.

"Oh, Moonhead," she repeated, "Moonhead."

Mukta touched her hand tenderly.

"It must be done," she said. "You're nearly finished." Mukta paused. "He had great courage. He lived beyond the grave of the sea in order to pass his stories on to us... to you, Teta. We should not judge him. You will, I think, find comfort in Moonhead's story of death. I will tell it to you before we sleep."

Teta bent once more over her task and, with a final dig and a powerful pull, she freed the tooth. She rubbed it on her sealskin and held it up to the moonlight.

"Put it away," Mukta ordered hoarsely. "Soogat is coming!"

Teta quickly cut a handful of Moonhead's hair. She thrust the tooth, the hair, and the stiletto into her pouch and began stroking Moonhead's arm.

✦✦✦✦✦✦

Soogat approached Teta warily. She seemed to be very involved with Moonhead's body. He wondered what she was doing, but he was afraid to anger her further by questioning her.

The fact that his mother sat with Teta pleased him, for Mukta would see to it that Teta did not try anything foolish.

He slowed his steps. All day he had been trying to find the right words to say to her. But she had glared at him, cutting his words off before they reached his tongue. He sighed wearily and shook his head. Before Moonhead had come to the Land of the Blue Rock, his life had been mapped out clearly. He was to become leader one day and Teta was to be his mate, once he had found where Lome had taken her. Now all that was changed. All because of Moonhead. Moonhead!

Mukta and Teta looked up as if waiting for him to do or say something. Teta's face tore at his soul. Her eyes were red and puffy and still sparkling with tears. Her expression was one of suspicion and loathing.

Wordlessly, torn between anger and guilt, he returned to the fire, where his men waited to find out how he was going to make good on his word about burying Moonhead face down in a grave.

Chapter Nine

Teta awoke as a hand on her shoulder shook her urgently. She sat up and rubbed her eyes. She had not slept well beside Moonhead's body, but she had refused to join Mukta in Soogat's tent.

Mukta was bending over her, holding a shell of steaming tea.

"Here, drink this," she said, kindly. "It is going to be a difficult morning for you. The men have been digging all through the night. I think they are almost finished."

Teta stood up and accepted the hot liquid. Her body ached.

"I wish they would all stop staring at me," she said to Mukta as three little girls sauntered past, their mouths hanging open, their eyes wide.

"It's to be expected," Mukta answered. "A chase always causes excitement. Your appearance in itself is a source of wonder." She faced Teta. "Over the last few days I've watched you closely. You've grown almost as cold and lifeless as Moonhead's body. Do not let this experience turn you hard, dear niece."

Teta shrugged and rotated her shoulders to loosen the tightness. For two days Soogat had marched them south. Finally, when they had located a patch of land where the earth would accept a grave, they waited for the South People to join them. They came eagerly, she knew, to witness Moonhead's burial and to obey their new leader. Just as much, they had come to stare at her, the girl who mated with the storyteller when she was plegded to their chief.

"I hate how they all crowd around the hole," Teta said, narrowing her eyes at the group of South People surrounding the burial site. "They can hardly wait to see what will happen next."

"You cannot blame them for being curious," Mukta said, smiling slightly. "And most of them are just as sad as you are. Some are grieving deeply. They knew him a lot longer than you did. Their favorite storyteller is dead."

Teta sipped on her berry tea. She did her best to ignore the gawking villagers and kept her eyes on Soogat.

Soogat and his ten plus nine men were busy digging, with only their heads and shoulders visible above ground. They had been at it for six days. The noise of the caribou antlers scooping out the dirt was deeply chilling to Teta. What was Soogat up to? This was not normal burial procedure! The hole, she could clearly see, measured the length of two men lying head to toe and three men wide.

At least Soogat had been too intent on his task to pay her much attention.

A big pile of sizable rocks and boulders lay in a heap to one side. An upside-down walrus skull sat beside the firepit. Teta took a few steps toward it and peered inside. It was filled with ochre dust. The bone used for grinding was stained red and lay on the ground.

"Soogat, what are you doing?" Teta called, hoping her shakiness did not show in her voice.

"Digging," came the sarcastic reply. The men laughed.

"I can see that," she retorted, gritting her teeth. "Why are you making such a big hole? Isn't it big enough?"

"I'm shaping the earth to look like the vessel Moonhead came in." Soogat shook out the stiff muscles of his arms. "This is about the right size. Stop digging."

One by one, the men scrambled out over the rim of the pit.

"Throw him in," cried Soogat.

"No! Stop!" A voice, strong and clear, made them all turn. Lome came striding across the stony tundra. "Do not throw him in."

Teta ran to him.

"Father. I am happy to see you," she said, flinging herself into his welcoming arms.

"What are you doing here, Lome, old uncle?" Soogat asked, a deep frown creasing his brow.

"I set out to follow my daughter and her mate." Lome smiled at Teta. By the tightness of Soogat's lips, Teta knew the jab had found its mark. "I had hoped not to find a gravedigging."

"I could just as easily have left his skinny body for the wolves and scavengers," Soogat snarled. "But my old mother insisted he be placed in the safety of the ground."

"If the size of a grave is a measure of its safety, then this is a very safe grave," Lome smiled wickedly at Mukta, who grinned back. They held each other in a warm embrace. "It's good to see you, sister."

Mukta nodded, her eyes brimming with her happiness.

Lome's eyes narrowed as he moved to Soogat's side. "Why are you doing this?"

"Because," Soogat replied, sticking his face close to Lome

for emphasis, "Moonhead was not like us. He will not be given the usual burial."

"Ah," Lome sighed. "So, it's a vengeful thing that you do. I thought perhaps..."

"I've heard enough talk," Soogat said, waving his uncle's words away.

He strode over to Moonhead's body. He stripped him of the blood-stained snow bear and body coverings until only the loin cloth remained. The old wound in Moonhead's side gaped raggedly.

He swirled. "Where is the Branch of the Talking Teeth?"

Teta held her breath. She knew everyone looked at her. Soogat, the snow bear hanging limply over one arm, marched up to her.

"Where's the branch?" he asked again, slowly and menacingly.

Teta swallowed and raised her eyes to his. They burned dark and furious in the bright light of the sun.

"Where is it?" Soogat shouted without moving his gaze.

Teta breathed deeply, trying to answer, but found herself trembling instead. Soogat grabbed a handful of her hair.

Teta cried out in pain. "I don't have it."

"I don't believe you," he yelled back. "He would have given it to you. I know he would."

"Let her go," ordered Lome. Soogat sent him a paralyzing stare.

"I don't have it," Teta said again, her neck bending sideways under the force of his grip.

"Give it to me or tell me where it is." Soogat's angry spittle showered the air between them. "Or I'll tear the clothes from your back to see for myself if you have it."

"Stop it." Lome tried to pull Soogat away. Soogat's men stepped forward and pushed him back.

"I told you, I don't have it," she stated, feeling the tears prick her eyelids. "You can do what you want with me, but I will never tell you where the branch is."

"I could kill you," he threatened.

Teta could tell it was an empty threat. She summoned her courage and glowered at him. Immediately, he let go of her hair.

"Yes, you could kill me," she said, shaking her head and rubbing her scalp. Suddenly, an idea came to her that drained the blood from her face. "But if you did that you would never find the branch and you could never mate with me. Allow me to keep the branch and I will honour the pledge my mother made to your mother."

"No, Teta," pleaded Lome.

"Teta," Mukta whispered in her ear, "you don't need to do this. The pledge doesn't need to be honoured now that you've bonded with Moonhead."

"Whose side are you on, old mother?" Soogat barked. Mukta backed away.

He turned his head so that he could see Teta out of the corner of his eye.

She stuck out her chin and waited.

Soogat pursed his mouth and considered Teta's proposal. He could hardly believe his ears. He would gladly have thrown himself on the ground in front of her and agreed to her conditions—until the image of her bonding with Moonhead swept into his mind.

"What makes you think I would want you now?" Soogat ran his eyes over her body. He had intended to make her uncomfortable, but succeeded only in fueling his desire for her.

Teta shrugged and glanced around the ring of onlookers. "My father has often visited the North People, my mother's people. Bonding with me would bring you new trade. There is no shame in bonding with a woman whose mate has died in battle. Also, *I, Teta,* now know the stories."

Looking directly at Soogat, she said, loudly. "I am the keeper of the Branch of the Talking Teeth. Surely, even you must understand how important Moonhead's legends have become to the People." She tossed her head. "Oh, I think you still want me."

Soogat let her insult pass. There was a much larger issue at stake.

"And you would give yourself to me, willingly, if I were to let you keep the branch?" Soogat asked. Inwardly he cringed at the eagerness in his voice. He had hoped to remain aloof.

Teta nodded once, her head barely moving.

Soogat shifted his weight. He folded his arms. Then he scratched the back of his head. All the while he studied her. She stood as still as one of those stone cairns. He admired her spirit. He glanced at his mother, who remained expressionless. He looked at Lome whose face seemed as grey as the thunder clouds before a storm. He walked around the circle of his silent people, and their barely contained excitement stirred him.

He decided to test Teta. He would touch her face. If she cringed or glared at him as she had these last few days, he would refuse her. She would be humiliated in front of her kin. She would have no choice but to go to the North People, or anywhere he sent her. Of course, he would first have the branch. But if she did not cringe...

He sent a silent prayer to the Goddess of All. "Please, don't let her cringe. I promise that if she doesn't cringe, I will be fair and good to her all my life."

He moved close to Teta. He could feel her breath coming in short pants against his throat. She lowered her eyelids. He saw how her lashes fanned out against her rosy cheeks. Soogat reached out his hand.

Teta closed her eyes and steeled herself. He was standing so near. She could feel the heat of his body. She knew he had raised his hand. His palm as it touched her skin was dry, not clammy as she had expected. His shaking fingers as they travelled across her eyebrows and over her lips were gentle. Her eyes flew open in surprise.

Soogat smiled broadly.

"I agree," he cried. "You of the South People, behold your leader's mate."

The people cheered. Mukta clasped her hands in delight. Lome sank onto the nearest boulder and cradled his head in his hands. Teta blinked and swallowed hard. She had sold herself to Soogat for the price of the Branch of the Talking Teeth and Moonhead's stories.

Soogat turned back to Teta. "Where is the branch? I want to see it."

"No." Teta said. "I won't show it to you until I feel you are ready."

Lome snorted. "That will never happen."

"Be quiet, old uncle. I'll be ready sooner than you think,"

Soogat said as he jumped into the hole. "Bring Moonhead to me." His order carried on the wind.

"Carefully," said Lome, lowering himself into the grave after Soogat. He carried the walrus skull.

The tears ran freely down Teta's cheeks as she watched Moonhead being jostled and manhandled. She shuddered as Soogat dragged the body over to one side of the pit.

"Watch," Soogat shouted to those ringing the hole. "This is how I found him lying in the boat."

In one swift, powerful move, Soogat rolled Moonhead's body over until it lay on its stomach, face turned slightly to the right.

"I don't remember. Was he face down in the boat?" Mukta asked. She slithered over the edge on her stomach, her legs dangling. She let go and landed with a soft thud.

"No," Soogat answered simply.

"Surely you're not going to leave him like that!" Lome cried in disbelief as he crossed the grave floor.

"Why not?" Soogat reached for the walrus skull. "He dishonoured me by bonding with my pledged mate."

"No, my son," Mukta interrupted, catching him by the arm. "Not even you can be so unkind as to bury a dead man face down. It is the burial of the shamed. He was not a man of shame."

Soogat ignored his mother, jerking free from her grasp.

"I've won," he chuckled. "I've achieved all that I wanted. Victory has brought with it power, and I am going to enjoy every moment."

He shook the walrus skull and showered Moonhead's body with the red ochre dust.

Back and forth, Soogat dusted the white skin. Teta watched as the white hair, the thighs, back, and shoulders became coated.

"There," he sighed, obviously happy with the results. "The great storyteller has entered his burial chamber." He folded his arms. "For some reason, I get pleasure from this farce."

"Shall we ask for guidance for him from the Goddess of All?" Mukta asked.

"Hah!" Soogat handed the empty skull to one of his men. "He didn't believe in our ways. You know that, old mother. Let his own spirits guide him."

Mukta covered her mouth with one hand.

Lome faced Soogat. "Move aside so we can leave our gifts. Or are you going to disgrace yourself as well as Moonhead with this burial?"

Soogat glared at Lome. "Leave your treasures for what good it will do."

Lome reached behind his back and brought forth a long, white walrus tusk. Carvings of fish and caribou circled the ivory.

"I had been saving this for my own grave," Lome said, looking up at Teta.

Each of Soogat's men placed a spear point or arrowhead at a shoulder, a foot, or an elbow. Some of the women left beads or shells.

"So, you've given him treasures and weapons to defend himself," Soogat said in a tone of authority. "He will need them. The Great Spirits will be angry at him for his meddling."

He looked up at Teta. "Do you have something you wish to leave here?"

Still numb from the bargain she had just made with Soogat, Teta dropped into the grave and walked slowly to Moonhead's side. She knelt down, removed her neck rope of birds' beaks, and draped it over his head. She leaned forward to speak in his ear.

"Moonhead, Mearanach, I know you can hear me. I will not forget the stories. I promise." She fingered her new neck rope of pebbles. "And I have the two Moonhead stones, one for your story of the beginning and one for your story of death. They will not be forgotten either."

She sat back on her heels. The body that lay there showed signs of decay. Moonhead was no more. For several heartbeats she recalled his laughter after their escapade with the wolves. She felt his smooth, white skin beneath her fingertips as she listened to his story of his coming to the Land of the Blue Rock. He had been with her for such a short while. He had almost been a dream.

Her attention shifted to Soogat. He heaved a large, flat piece of rock over to Moonhead's body. She cried out as he lowered it, none too gently, onto Moonhead's back.

"There," he said, brushing the sand from his palms. "This body will never rise. I never have to look at the face of Moonhead again."

He climbed out of the hole and commanded everyone else to follow. Teta, the last to leave, felt the sprinkle of sand from Soogat's antler shovel.

◆◆◆◆◆

The waves were licking the face of the night before the hole was filled again. Soogat seemed tireless as he piled the rocks over the top.

Lome sat nearby and beat a steady rhythm on his skin drum. Teta sat beside him, rocking in time. Mukta looked on, shaking her head.

"Where is the Branch of the Talking Teeth, Teta?" Lome asked under his breath when Soogat was farthest from them.

"Hidden in the furs of the dead Aurtoo. Soogat will not look there. It was Mukta's idea." Teta wiped her wet cheeks with her sleeve. The fingers of her other hand played constantly with her Moonhead Stones.

Lome did not answer. He continued his drumming.

Soogat ran to his tent and brought back Moonhead's walking stick. He examined the engravings intently before scrambling to the top of the mound. He placed the walrus skull on the walking stick and wedged it between the highest rocks.

"Moonhead told me the tree in the middle of the boat was called a mast." Soogat shouted against the driving wind. "Here is Moonhead's mast."

Soogat threw back his head and laughed. Teta shut her eyes tightly against the harsh sound.

"Let's eat," he cried, picking his way down. "I've worked up a huge hunger."

Teta did not go with the others for the meal of shellfish and dried berries. She wanted to be alone.

She walked some distance from the twinkling warmth of the fire. As she sat on a boulder, the wind tugged at her hair and stung her tear-misted eyes. She stared at the stars as they drifted in and out of the gathering sea mist. She shivered against the pounding of the waves, thinking of everything and of nothing.

Mukta came up behind her and dropped a fur skin over her shoulders.

"Here, girl," she said softly. "Take old Aurtoo's covering for some warmth. Come to the fire when you're ready."

Teta felt something drop in her lap. She looked down to see the Branch of the Talking Teeth.

"You'll need to prepare yourself, daughter of Lome," Mukta

sighed. "Jaanu, our Woman of Wisdom, is dead. The People need a new Wise One. Lome has taught you well and you know our stories. I think you should become our new Woman of Wisdom."

With that, Mukta shuffled away.

Teta brought her lips together in a hard line. The new Woman of Wisdom? Her?

Before Moonhead had thrown his shadow over her, before she had walked with him, she would have argued with anyone who suggested she become a Woman of Wisdom. But now, having known a kind and gentle man, having learned his people's messages, having seen the cruelness that can spread like fog, smothering the goodness in people, she felt wise, almost old.

As Soogat's mate she would hold the position of counsellor as well as mate. As the Woman of Wisdom she would even have control over Soogat. These thoughts both fortified and terrified her.

First, she needed to create a story.

She ran her fingers along the branch, stopping to caress Moonhead's tooth, hung by its braided white hair, next to the tooth of Labhradair.

Teta lifted the branch and rattled it at the wind.

This is the story of the seventh tooth, the tooth of Moonhead, Mearanach. He believed in the power of stories.

The End

In 1973, Robert McGhee and James Tuck, working for the Memorial University of Newfoundland, arrived on the south coast of Labrador to investigate archeological sites in that area. They stumbled upon a pile of rocks which stimulated their imaginations so much that they returned to excavate it the following year.

After days of hard work and digging, the skeleton of an adolescent of about thirteen was unearthed. Strangely, the young boy had been buried on his stomach instead of on his back. The face was turned to one side and a large slab of rock lay on his back. Among the grave offerings was a walrus tusk, several spear points, a bone pendant, an antler harpoon head, and a bird bone-whistle.

McGhee estimates that it would have taken approximately twenty people digging with caribou antlers a week to complete this grave. Radiocarbon dates confirm the burial happened between 7000-7500 years ago. This site at L'Anse-Amour is among the oldest of its kind known anywhere on earth.

McGhee proposes several theories as to why a child was buried in such an unusual position. He also invites us to rely on imagination rather than archeological fact for answers. So I did. I simply took the unearthed evidence and fabricated a story. If by doing so, I bring to the reader some sense of early human history, or awaken some curiosity about our origins, then all the better. But I must stress that this book is a work of pure fiction.

When I was "discovering" the characters for this book and their names, I recalled that there is an ancient Celtic legend of

Labra the Mariner. Labhradair (orator), Mearanach (moon-struck), Cuimhne (memory), Sneachda (snow), and kuruko (boat) are all Gaelic (old Scottish) words. The Labhradair/Labrador similarity was too much for me to overlook.

I also noted a similarity between the dwellings of ancient Labrador, Canada, and those in Scotland from the same time. Perhaps the idea of people travelling west from early Europe, across the treacherous sea and snow-packed islands of the North Atlantic, is not so far-fetched.

Irish master poets are said to have carried *The Silver Branch*—a straight branch strung with nine silver bells. This branch served as an inspiration, helping the poet to remember and commune with the "other world." For my story, I needed something older than silver, something that rattled as if talking from the other world. Teeth were readily available to people down through the ages. Thus was created **The Branch of the Talking Teeth**.

The great silver wolf as it is portrayed in this story is an element of fantasy. The author in no way wishes to contribute to the malignment of the modern-day wolf.

Ishbel Moore was born in Scotland and emigrated as a teenager to Canada with her family in 1967. She is married and has three school-aged children. She lives in Winnipeg, Manitoba. Her love of history is an integral part of her writing.

Ms. Moore is the two-time recipient of the Canadian Authors Short Fiction, Manitoba Branch, Award for 1993 and 1994.

MARQUIS

PRINTED BY
IMPRIMERIE D'ÉDITION MARQUIS
IN MAY 1995
MONTMAGNY (QUÉBEC)